# MIDNIG...

## BY
## KAREN KENDALL

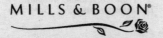

MILLS & BOON®

*First published in Great Britain 2007
by Harlequin Mills & Boon Limited,
Eton House, 18-24 Paradise Road, Richmond, Surrey TW9 1SR*

© Karen Moser 2006

*ISBN: 978 0 263 85585 2*

*14-0807*

*Printed and bound in Spain
by Litografia Rosés S.A., Barcelona*

## KAREN KENDALL

has always been fascinated by people who don't do what other people expect them to – people who play odd roles in life. So maybe it was natural for her to write about a guy who has a funny secret and a girl who's trying to break free of family expectations. After all, Karen's favourite question is "What if...?" Because of that very question, she's now the author of twelve romantic comedies and shows disturbing signs of wanting to write many more!

With thanks to all my Florida friends who have brightened my new life here! And especially to Sandra, Adolfo, Hugo, Carla and Stany for helping me get the cultural details/Spanish straight. I couldn't have written this book without you.

# 1

*IF WORD GETS out, I'm a dead man.*

Alejandro Torres looked furtively behind him to make sure he wasn't spotted; then ducked into the backroom of After Hours. A real man wouldn't live this way, slipping into the darkness, blending with the shadows, unable to reveal to anyone what he did for a living.

He told himself that CIA operatives were in the same boat, but unfortunately there was one key difference: ops guys carried concealed weapons and cool gadgets. Alejandro carried a concealed pumice stone and very *un*cool purple foam toe separators.

CIA agents—in theory—sought to protect truth, justice and the American way. Alejandro sought to protect his machismo: keep his cojones from shriveling to the size of peas and dropping off into the dust.

His code name was Señor Manos. Not quite 007, but then, this wasn't MI6—After Hours was an upscale salon and day spa in Coral Gables, one of the ritzier sections of Miami.

It was way too hot for a cloak, and he'd never needed a dagger yet, but the secrecy was urgent. Alejandro shuddered. If any of his buddies on the soccer team found out what he was up to, things wouldn't be pretty. He should never, ever have filled in for that MIA nail technician!

It was one thing to be a financial partner in a spa. It was quite another for a six-foot-four Peruvian male to be a closet manicurist. But there seemed to be no turning back now: he was in demand, even at the outrageous prices he'd begun charging to dissuade appointments.

"Señor Manos," said a high, breathy female voice. "I've been waiting all week for this."

The voice came from the shadows of the pedicure chair, from behind a pair of tanned, candlelit knees that were *not* pressed firmly together.

In fact, the knees were a foot apart from one another, which was alarming, since they wore a short skirt. Not that Alejandro hadn't spread his share of female knees in his thirty-four years—he certainly had. But he didn't wish to spread this pair, not even a little bit. Those were married knees. Knees of a three-time mother.

Nevertheless, as a salon and spa owner, he was accomplished at lying to women. Just part of doing business. "And I, *mi corazon,* have also been waiting all week. You have toes to melt a man."

The client giggled. "Oh, honey. Do I really have man-melting toes? I don't believe anyone's ever said that to me."

"Then you have obviously been with the wrong men." He smiled and seated himself on the low stool in front of the basin area of her pedicure chair. "How's the water temperature?" He dipped his hands in.

"It just got hotter, thanks." She giggled again, and then sighed with pleasure as he took her left foot in his hands and tried not to stare up her skirt, which was quite difficult.

His balls had sagged immediately as he assumed the position. They drooped in shame as he began a preliminary massage with soft liquid soap—an extra service that After Hours provided to their clients.

Heather Carlton, the woman in his chair, moaned with pleasure and Alejandro's manhood pulled a complete turtle, retreating from the horror of this abasement and servitude.

He actually didn't mind the foot massage, as long as the foot in question wasn't too large and gruesome. It was scrubbing the calluses, pushing back the cuticles, cleaning under the nails and filing them that he really despised. And the polishing.

Bad enough that he knew how to do all of it, having grown up helping out in his mother's salon. Beauty Boy, the kids at school had called him, taunting him mercilessly. On one particular, ignominious afternoon, a gang of bullies had jumped him after classes, beaten him to a pulp and then decked him out in a wig and a full face of makeup. He'd laid there groaning until he could force himself up and find a gas station restroom so he could wash it all off.

His mama had scolded him and grounded him for fighting, but he'd never told her what really happened. She was a single mother in a country not her own, and he was all she had, besides her partner and best friend

Carlotta Perez. He didn't want Mama to feel guilty that he had to help her after school and on weekends.

Heather's moans of bliss subsided as he rinsed her feet and applied a grainy scrub to exfoliate them and slough off dead skin cells.

"You really have magic hands," she said.

"*Gracias.*"

"How did a big, handsome guy like you become a nail technician? I can't figure it out."

Alejandro laughed. "By accident. My family's been in the salon business for years." *And now, even though Mama's passed on, I can't seem to get away from it, since Tia Carlotta has no retirement savings and needs me to turn a tidy profit for her….*

Those were the things that he couldn't say aloud. The issues that explained why he was stuck in the particular rut of life he found himself in. There were other things he couldn't say, either. Such as:

*I hate doing this and that's why I'm getting an MBA on the side. But until I'm done with school and figure out how to franchise After Hours in every big city in the U.S., I have to meet client demands. If the clients are demanding my touch, and will pay as much as you're paying for me to lay my* magic hands *on you, then so be it.*

Heather drained her free glass of wine and hinted strongly that she'd like another. After Hours, to Tia Carlotta's great suspicion, served alcohol and was open until midnight Tuesday through Saturday. He'd bought out most of her interest, relocated the old salon, renamed it and given it a new marketing twist.

Miami was a late-night, party town. They needed to cater to their clientele, and giving them a hot, pre-party spot to get beautiful and tipsy was the perfect solution. The tipsier the clients got, the happier they were and the more money they spent.

Alejandro rose from his stool and held out his hand for her glass. In Peru, his mother's country, the women waited on the men. "Chardonnay or pinot grigio, *mi amorcito?*"

"Ooh, say that again."

"Say what?" Alejandro asked. *"Mi amorcito?"*

"Well, I like that, too, of course. But the other."

"Pinot grigio?"

"Yes. It sounds so sexy when you say it." She sighed and stretched, flashing him abundant cleavage and a swatch of emerald-green crotch.

*Crazy woman.* "Pinot grigio," Alejandro repeated, averting his gaze. "Is that what you would like, then? Not the chardonnay?"

"Grinot pigio," she said. "Yes, please. *Mi*, uh, *corazon.*"

He bit his lip to keep from laughing. Maybe she was drunker than he'd thought. "Of course. I'll be back in a moment."

He opened the door and slipped out, leaving her alone with the ocean wave music, the candlelight and her wine-buzz. All clear in the hallway. He straightened his shoulders and headed for the little coffee-and-wine area up front, where the customers could help themselves.

For liability reasons, Alejandro and the staff were careful not to serve more than one or two glasses of wine. After that, if the client wanted more, it was available on a self-service basis.

"Are you drinking on the job again?" his partner Marly teased him, as he poured Heather's wine. She was the salon's master hairdresser, and had recently become engaged to Florida's governor, Jack Hammersmith.

"Always, *mi vida*." He winked. "Actually, my client just asked me for a glass of grigot pinio. No, grinot pigio."

Marly laughed. "Pinot grigio?"

"Well, that's what she meant to say."

"I think Heather was lit when she came in here," their tiny blond receptionist, Shirlie, reported from behind the checkout counter. "She sorta rolled through the door. And I also think she wants you, Alejandro." Shirlie snapped her gum and grinned.

"There's a newsflash." Marly's voice was dry. "Yet another spoiled Coral Gables housewife panting after our Alejo."

He hunched his shoulders. It was actually getting embarrassing, the number of female clients who were trying to bed him.

Nicky, another hairstylist, skipped up and sang into a faux fist microphone, making up the lyrics as he went along. "Yo touch, baby, yo touch, it's just tooooo much!" He followed that with an air-guitar riff. Then he folded his hands behind his head and gyrated his pelvis. Alejandro averted his gaze from the painful sight.

"Nicky, don't quit your day job, okay?"

"You'll be sorry when I'm the next American Idol, sweets."

Alejandro retreated with the wine, calling over his shoulder, "If you ever even pass the first round of *American Idol,* I will eat an entire box of your high-lighting foil."

"Fine," Nicky shouted after him, hands on his black, leather-encased hips. "You better work up an appetite for aluminum, then."

Alejandro did a quick scan of the hallway and then ducked back into the treatment room. He refused to sit out in front with the other manicurists, because of the risk of being seen by someone he knew. He'd only sat out there a couple of times before deciding that he'd never live it down if one of the guys on his soccer team walked by on his way to Benito's restaurant and got an eyeful of their star forward with a bottle of nail polish.

Forget Beauty Boy. They'd call him *maricon*—fag— or *chivo,* an even ruder Peruvian term that meant *goat.* They'd also run him right off the team, talent be damned.

Heather had slid even farther down into the chair, which had caused her skirt to hike up several inches. Not for the first time, Alejandro wondered if he shouldn't just swallow his pride and move up to the front with the others. It would save him from would-be seduction scenes like this one. *Beauty Boy! Beauty Boy!* The old taunt echoed through his head. He just couldn't do it.

"Your wine, *señora.*" He handed Heather the glass.

"No, no, please don't call me that—it makes me feel a hundred years old."

*And it reminds you that you're a married mother of*

*three. Tsk, tsk.* "Apologies, *mi amorcito.* If it's any comfort, you look all of twenty-two."

"Now you're talking, honey."

Alejo assumed the position again and began sawing away at the calluses on Heather's feet, while she sat shamelessly flashing her emerald-green crotch and a come-hither smile.

He wasn't coming any more hither than he already was. He rinsed off her feet, dried them, drained the basin and began her foot and calf massage with scented lotion. She began to make little noises of pleasure, soft moans and small mewls, while he ignored her and tried to be professional.

Once he was done, he wiped his hands on a towel, removed the lotion residue from her toenails and adjusted the light so that he could see better. Heather returned to her wine, blinking resentfully at the stronger light.

She'd chosen a dark red polish color called Sex on the Subway. Coincidence? He thought not. Who were the people who made up these cosmetic colors, anyway?

Alejandro applied two coats to her toenails and then topped it with a clear polish, while she managed to drain the second glass of wine in record time. She stared at him through slitted, smoky eyes that she'd taken great pains making up.

He was cleaning up the last toe on her right foot with a wooden cuticle stick and a bit of acetone when she said huskily, "What ish thish thing between us, Alejandro?"

Alarmed, he repeated, "Thing?"

Then she lurched forward and stuck her left foot, wet polish and all, into his crotch. "Oh, baby! Is that a python in your pants?"

He looked down, his jaw working. Red nail polish—all over his trousers. He searched for tact. *Remember, she's a client.*

She blinked at the mess, giggled and covered her mouth with a hand. "Oops. Sorry…"

He gently removed her foot and wiped her ruined toenails with a paper towel soaked in acetone. He didn't bother with his pants—they were history. "*Señora,* I think the wine may have gone to your head."

She put a hand on her heart. "No, it hasn't. I feel this 'lectricity in the air when I'm with you, and I can tell you feel the shame way." She glanced meaningfully at his, er, python, which wasn't feeling at all aggressive. In fact, it had practically shrunk up to his chin.

He had to step carefully. "Indeed, *señora,* you are very beautiful, and a man would have to be dead not to, ah, desire you. However, you are a married woman and a mother—I could not possibly act on such an attraction. It cannot be." There, was that dramatic and mournful enough? He hoped so.

"Just because I have kids doesn't mean I'm *dead.*" To his horror, Heather began to cry.

He stared at her, aghast.

"You think I'm a tramp, don't you?"

"No, no, no, no, no! I think you're a lovely lady," Alejandro said desperately. "Really."

"You think I'm ugly."

"No! You are gloriously, stunningly beautiful."

"Then you think I'm fat." Tears rolled down her cheeks.

"I do not think you're fat. You're like a—" he searched wildly "—a gazelle!"

"Now you're calling me an animal?"

"It was a compliment! Gazelle—you know, graceful. Svelte! *Dainty.*"

"You don't *waaaaaaant* me," she moaned.

"I do. I want you, Heather, more than—than words can say. Madly. Passionately."

"You do?"

He nodded, his hand over his heart. "But first, we must paint your toenails, yes?"

She gave a woeful sniff. "Uh-huh."

"Excellent. Now, give me your scrumptious foot, *mi corazon.* Let me make it as lovely as the rest of you."

Heather stuck out her foot and her lip at the same time while he thought wildly of what disease or disability to claim so that he could get out of this mess.

She sulked for a while.

*Syphilis? Or erectile dysfunction? Eeny meeny miny mo, catch a whopper by its toe...please, lady, just let me go!*

Then the heavens intervened. "By the way, you should know that I'm not really in the mood anymore, Alejandro."

*Praise God and all His angels.* Alejo dredged up a wounded expression. "But...I am devastated."

She shrugged and tossed her hair over her shoulder. Then she folded her arms across her chest and pressed her knees firmly together. If he hadn't been so relieved, he might have poked his eyes out with the cuticle stick.

*Women.* Hard enough to understand them when they were sober. He couldn't keep up with their lightning changes of mood then, much less adding alcohol to the equation. All he knew was that he'd been spared, thanks be to Jesus.

Alejandro polished Heather's toes for the second time that night, and then escaped from the room, only to run into Peggy Underwood, his other partner.

Peg, the spa's massage therapist, stuck her hands into the pockets of her white lab coat and looked pointedly at his crotch. Her eyebrows climbed into her hair. "Alejo, did your client try to Bobbitt you?"

He could feel his face sizzling. "No. She, um…"

"Tried to play footsie with your tootsie?"

"That about covers it."

Peggy grinned. "Sweetie, it's gotten to the point where we can tell which women are your clients. The ones who come in for their pedicures in short skirts. They're absolutely shameless!"

"Yeah, tell me about it. I can't keep doing this, Peggy. If my buddies find out…" He shook his head.

"Alejandro. Since you've been doing pedicures, our revenue on them has shot sky-high. Like it or not, your fifty-dollar pedicures are bringing in over two thousand dollars a week, and don't tell me to hire someone else, because it's *you* they want. Shirlie tells me we get calls all the time, asking for the guy who looks like Jesse Metcalfe from *Desperate Housewives.* If you're not available, they say they'll wait."

"But it's humiliating!" he complained. "You don't understand. Peruvian men don't give manicures or pedicures. They just don't! You have no idea what will happen if this gets out. I will be branded *rosquete,* be the butt of jokes, kicked off the soccer team!"

"What's a *rosquete?*" Peggy asked.

Alejandro shuddered. "It's very rude. It means big doughnut, and it's used to describe gay men."

Peg snorted with laughter.

"It's not funny!" he hissed. "Not at all."

"Sorry," she said, trying and failing to smother her mirth.

"I'm telling you, I cannot do this anymore."

She sobered. "Alejo, it's just until we get the business loans paid down. You said it yourself."

"Yes, and my MBA loan, and— There's no end in sight. Meanwhile I'm dying inside every time I touch a woman's foot or hand!"

"Sweetie, how many men would beg to be mauled by beautiful women all day long?"

He growled.

"Plenty of Asian men do nails. Why shouldn't you?"

He growled again.

"I know, I know. But we'll keep your secret. None of the clients even know your real name, Señor Manos, and your friends just think you're an owner. It will be fine. Our secret. Just for a few more months."

He groaned and swiped a hand over his face. "You don't understand. *Latino men do not give manicures!*"

## 2

THE NEXT MORNING, Alejandro sat in dark slacks and a pressed white shirt in his marketing class, one of the requirements for the Executive MBA program at the University of Miami.

As usual, his gaze strayed from the professor's scintillating discussion of economics to the profile of Kate Spinney, a fellow classmate.

Kate's face was all angles and planes and chiseled features—like a young Katharine Hepburn. Even in her baggy, frayed khaki pants and oversize man's blue oxford shirt, her feet stuck into beat-up, brown penny loafers, Kate was gorgeous. And as far as he could tell, completely unaware of her looks.

Penny loafers. God, they were ugly! Women in Miami did not wear such things. They wore high-heeled, strappy, sexy sandals. They wore ankle bracelets and toe rings. They did not wear men's shoes or shapeless clothing.

But Alejandro had observed Kate for months now, and he couldn't imagine her in sexy, strappy heels or low-slung, skintight pants that bared her belly.

When it came to fashion, she was a walking disaster,

and when it came to social grace… His mouth twisted wryly. Kate certainly hadn't been born in the South.

At the meet-and-greet cocktail party that kicked off the first semester of the program, she'd stood forlornly in her loafers, clutching a bottle of beer in her scrawny hands. She'd shredded the label using her ragged, un-polished nails within minutes, and she shook hands like a man: no nonsense, vice-like grip, brief nod and sketchy introduction. "Hi, I'm Kate Spinney from Boston."

No, "A pleasure to make your acquaintance," or "Nice to meet you." Just the identifying tag and the im-personal hand-squeeze. That was Kate.

She had the intellectual capacity of a mainframe computer, and Alejandro wondered why she wasn't studying business at Harvard or Yale or Wharton. Over-all, she seemed the sort of person who belonged in Miami about as much as a hooker belonged in a convent.

He was curious; intrigued. And he didn't know why, since his tastes in women usually ran to black hair, C-cup and size eight. Kate had springy, crazy, ginger-brown hair, tiny breasts that he'd guess were an A-minus and she'd be lucky to be a size two. In short, she was built like a string mop. And yet…he thought about her.

She wasn't an everyday, average woman, and he'd detected a hidden sense of humor behind her Yankee reserve. Every once in a while her green eyes went warm and sparkled with a sense of the ridiculous, etching lines of sweetness around her mouth. There was more to Kate than met the eye.

He turned his attention back to Professor Kurtz, a big burly guy with small eyes in a slab of face. But Alejandro couldn't stop his eyes from wandering back over Kate's messy, wiry curls and the way they clung to her delicate neck.

Kurtz was waxing poetic on the intricacies of supply and demand, using a certain brand of baby lotion as an example when Kate called out, "Excuse me, but that's incorrect."

All eyes in the small auditorium swiveled to her, and then to Kurtz and then back to her.

The professor bristled. "What do you mean, incorrect?"

"I mean that your information is wrong. In 2002, Johnson & Johnson wasn't even marketing that product."

"My information is reliable."

"Johnson didn't put that new lotion formula onto the shelves until spring of 2003. They were still product-testing in 2002. I know this because Spinney Industries is their main competitor, and we introduced our version of that lotion in October of 2001, gaining the edge in the market."

Kurtz blinked his small eyes rapidly. After a pause, he said, "Fine. Thank you, Miss Spinney."

"You're welcome. And it's Ms., please."

A collective rustle went through the class, some students hiding grins and snickers behind their hands. Kate appeared oblivious to this and the glare that Kurtz sent in her direction. She just swung her loafer-clad foot over her knee and bounced it gently as the lecture went on.

When she got tired of that position and put her feet flat on the ground, flexing them, Alejandro saw that the side stitching of her loafer had pulled free, leaving the sole flapping open and baring her little toe. Kate Spinney of the Spinney Industries family couldn't afford new shoes?

Ridiculous. The watch on her wrist was Tiffany, and he'd also seen her wear a Piaget. Her purse, though it was battered and worn, was an Hermès Kelly bag, which cost thousands of dollars new.

He found the sight of her little toe oddly endearing. She propped her chin on one hand and seemed entirely unconcerned that she'd just embarrassed their professor in front of the class.

From his position in the row behind her, he could see her doodling in the margins of her yellow pad. So far he could make out a bicycle, a sailboat and a beach umbrella. Literal, no-nonsense drawings, very illustrative of Kate's personality. He squinted to make out what she was sketching now, and chuckled when he saw a steak with eyes and legs. It looked uncannily like Professor Kurtz.

"Mr. Torres? Do you have something to add to the lecture?" the professor asked sharply.

Kate, along with a few others, turned and looked at him. So she knew who he was… He winked at her. She blinked, then raised a corner of her mouth uncertainly and turned back around.

"No, no. I just had something in my throat," Alejo said to Kurtz. "Sorry."

The professor pontificated some more with no further interruptions, and soon the class drew to an end.

"You'll be pairing up next week to begin the big semester project," he told them. "So keep that in mind. And please read chapters four through seven in your text."

Alejandro followed Kate out of the room and caught up with her easily in the hallway. "Kate? I admire you for speaking up back there."

She turned to face him, her green eyes wary over her high, aristocratic cheekbones. "Thank you." She edged away a couple of steps.

He closed the gap again. "I was wondering if you'd like to work together on Kurtz's project." He smiled down at her.

Surprise danced along those high cheekbones. Then her lips curved, and he caught a glimpse of a possible imp under her cool facade. "Are you sure you want to throw your fate in with mine? Kurtz doesn't like me much, especially not after today."

"I'm not worried about that. So what do you say?"

She took another step back from him, and he realized that she was used to more personal space. He didn't move any closer this time.

"What's your background and experience?" she asked, all business.

Now she was starting to annoy him a little. That nose in the air, her head cocked as if to use the cheekbones for weapons. "My background and experience? I've worked in my, uh…family business since I was about eight years old. And I have a university degree in finance." He looked a challenge at her. "What's yours?"

"I interned for years at Spinney Industries, worked

full time there for three years. Before that I earned a BA at Harvard, in English."

"Oh. *Harvard*." Alejandro clicked his tongue. "Then I'm afraid I can't possibly work with you on the project." He shook his head regretfully.

Her brow beetled. "Why not?"

"It's just not up to my standards. I'd be slumming." He kept a straight face as he met her gaze.

"Slumming?" she said, her tone incredulous. "I beg your pardon?"

"No need."

She made a strangled noise, and he grinned at her. "I'm feeling very egalitarian today, though. I might be willing to have a cup of coffee with you, even though you come from such a no-account family."

Her mouth worked for a moment and then she laughed. His gamble had paid off: Kate did have a hidden sense of humor. "I'm so flattered."

"Don't let it go to your head. So, caffeine? We have fifteen minutes before statistics class." He put a hand on her back to steer her forward, but she stiffened immediately. Apparently Ms. Spinney didn't like to be touched. Alejandro removed his hand and she took a deep breath. Interesting.

They walked across the street to a little coffee house, where he discovered that Kate liked her coffee black, just like he did. She pulled a wallet out of her beat-up bag and tried to pay for hers.

"No, no," he said. "I'll get this."

"You don't have to buy my coffee."

"I want to."

"No, really—"

"I am buying your coffee, Kate," he said with finality. He didn't care if, as a Spinney, she probably had a personal net worth bigger than the entire tax base of Peru. He stepped in front of her and put five dollars on the counter. Then he looked down at her little toe, poking out of its loafer. He winked at her. "You need to save your money for new shoes."

Her mouth opened and closed, and then a tide of red washed over her face. "I can afford new shoes. I just happen to like these. They're comfortable. Broken in."

"Is that what you call it?" From his superior height, Alejo noticed that one ear poked out of her untidy curls, and even the tip of it was red. "Because you may have noticed that your little piggy, there, is well on its way to the market."

Her lips twitched in spite of her obvious embarrassment. "No, you've got it wrong. Remember, it's the big toe that goes to market. The little one runs all the way home."

"Right, I'd forgotten. Well, the poor little guy has a ways to go, if he's running the whole distance back to Boston." He handed her one of the paper cups of coffee.

"Thank you. And he just ran *away* from Boston, so he's not likely to be running back there anytime soon. But I appreciate your concern." She took a sip of the coffee, her eyes glinting very green in the morning sunlight.

Alejandro eyed her over the rim of his own cup, as he drank some. "And why did he run away? How did he end up in Miami, of all places?"

His teasing had relaxed her some, since she blew out a breath and said, "Well, the other nine toes in the family shoe were cramping his style a bit. So the little piggy skipped off to business school as far away as possible." She gave him a wobbly smile.

She was so…adorably uptight. Alejandro wondered what it took for Kate Spinney to relax. He wondered if she relaxed in bed, and what that fragile body looked like naked. Athletic, he guessed.

She seemed edgy just talking in the abstract about her family. So he changed the subject. "Well, some of us are glad that the little piggy ended up here in Miami. She's awfully cute."

Red washed over her face again. "I think you gave her a sex change," she said dryly. "And I've been warned about smooth-talking Latin men like you."

It was his turn to stiffen. "I'm half Peruvian, half American," Alejandro said. "And we *smooth talkers* don't like to be referred to as Latin. We're from individual countries, and don't appreciate them being lumped all together."

"Sorry."

"About calling me a smooth talker, or a Latin?"

"A Latin."

He smiled. "That's okay. You didn't know."

"You *are* a smooth talker."

He lifted an eyebrow. "Why, thank you. I do other things smoothly, too, *mi corazon.*"

"And a flirt."

Alejandro found a table and pulled out a chair for her. "I stand accused of terrible crimes. I'm guessing they don't flirt at Harvard?"

She sat down gingerly, almost suspiciously.

"No, of course not," he said, deliberately provoking her. "Yankees don't know how to flirt."

"We do, too—"

"Well, then, Ms. Spinney, I hereby challenge you to a flirt-off."

She snorted into her coffee cup. "A flirt-off?"

He nodded. "Yes. And if I win, you have to buy a new pair of shoes—shoes of my choice."

"What if I win?"

"You won't. I'm a professional."

"We'll see about that."

"Like I said, it's not going to happen. So you really shouldn't worry your pretty little head over it, Kate," he said, doing his best to wind her up.

"As we've discussed, my pretty little head," she replied in ominous tones, "is Harvard-educated and dislikes patronizing men." But she softened the statement with a reluctant smile.

"Maybe so, but you don't have the slightest idea how to flirt. Flirting requires charm, and you're no southern belle. It's one of the things I like about you."

Her green eyes narrowed at him. "How do you *do* that?"

"Do what?"

"Say things that are insulting and then turn them around?"

"We smooth-talking Latins just have a way with words." Alejandro grinned at her, loving the outraged expression on her face. She looked very sexy when outraged. In fact, if she were to ditch the awful pants and unspeakable loafers and sit there barefoot in just the shirt…maybe unbutton it a few more inches so that it hung off one shoulder….

Kate looked at her watch. "We have to get back. We're going to be late."

"That's another thing you'll have to learn about, now that you live in Miami. Living on Latin time, *la hora latina.* We are always late. Without exception."

"That drives me crazy. It's so rude!"

"You'll have to get used to it, if you're going to hang out with me, *amorcito.*"

"What did you just call me? And who says I'm going to hang out with you?" But her lips twitched.

Alejandro drained his coffee and stood. He took their cups and dropped them in the trash. "I just called you *little love,* and of course you're going to hang out with me. We're going to work on the project together."

"I haven't agreed to that yet…."

"Well, no. But you will," he said calmly.

Her eyes flashed. "Oh, yeah? You're awfully sure of yourself, sport."

He nodded. "You're shy, Kate. I've watched you and you haven't mingled much. Do you even know anyone else well enough to ask them?"

She started walking faster, her beat-up loafers making clopping noises on the pavement. The sole of her left one flapped with each step, flashing her little toe.

"Hey," he said gently, and put a hand on her arm. She stopped, but wouldn't look at him. "It's not a criticism, you know."

"Most people say I'm stuck up or standoffish. How can you say I'm shy when I told Kurtz he was wrong in front of the whole class?"

"Ah, but that's different. It has to do with facts and figures, with intellect. You're very sure of your brains, Kate. It's socially that you're inhibited."

Her arm quivered slightly, and once again, she stepped away, creating space between them. "I appreciate your analysis, Doctor. Can I get off the couch, now?"

He had a sudden image of her lying naked on his brown leather sofa at home, wearing nothing but that little crease between her eyebrows. He wanted to get her off, all right.

"Thanks for the coffee," she said. "I'll think about the project and let you know." And Kate spun on her battered heel and walked quickly to the nearby ladies' room, where he couldn't follow her.

Alejandro tried not to stare at her ass as she pulled open the door, but failed miserably. He might be moonlighting as a manicurist right now, but he was still, after all, a man and not a *rosquete.*

He was also determined to work with Ms. Spinney on the marketing project. Because she intrigued and piqued him...and he knew instinctively that it was the only way to get into her baggy khaki pants.

# 3

KATE STARED OUT at the Atlantic Ocean from the window of her Key Biscayne condo and reveled in her loneliness. She didn't know a soul in the high-rise, and she rather liked it that way. All her life people had known her by her name, her parentage, her family.

Here in Miami she could blend in and be anonymous. Oh, there were countless acquaintances she could call if she wanted to tap into a built-in social network, but she didn't. She wanted to break out of the Spinney mold and just be a regular person, live a regular life.

As she watched the waves cresting on the shore, she thought about the gorgeous, slick Latin guy in her marketing class. He was funny and she half-liked him, even though he set off all kinds of warning bells in her head.

He was too good-looking, and too charming. But he was also intelligent and had unerringly taken the right tack with her. Kate was used to people tiptoeing around her family name and money; treating her with a certain amount of deference or awe—unless, of course, they came from the same type of background, in which case they didn't give a damn.

But Alejandro had mocked her instead of deferring

to her, which was refreshing, not to mention amusing. She wiggled her bare toes on the hardwood floors and glanced at her beat-up loafers. Her father would call them disgraceful and her mother wouldn't notice. Her brother wouldn't care. And Gerta, her parents' housekeeper, would make her leave them in the mudroom.

*You need to save your money for new shoes,* Alejandro had said to her, knowing full well that she was a Spinney and that her family's business supported entire towns. And he'd insulted Harvard. The corners of her mouth turned up. He had a nerve, didn't he? She liked that about him. She hated people who kissed her ass.

She wasn't sure she liked his flirting, though. And she didn't like her body's response to his touch. She didn't trust him. But that was nothing new—she hadn't been brought up to trust anyone.

"Don't be naive," her father had told her from the time she was ten. "You've been born a very wealthy little girl. People—and later, men in particular—will try to use you for your money."

Kate watched an opportunistic seagull dive and snatch something from the water before wheeling away. She envied its freedom—but more than that, she envied that the bird knew what to do with it.

She'd created some freedom by leaving Boston and putting hundreds of miles between herself and her family, but it still felt peculiar. She did a lot of rambling on her own, felt lonely much of the time, and second-guessed her decision to leave. But it was time.

The poor little rich girl: oldest story in the book. And yet she lived it, cliché that it was. Money was supposed to create freedom, wasn't it? Yet all too often it tied people down. Tied them to a certain lifestyle, or ways of thinking, or to a monolithic business dedicated to making more and more of the green stuff. And for what purpose? So that it could be counted, guarded, fought over, invested, lost or stolen.

Filthy lucre: that was how she'd come to think of it. Most of her family loathed each other or didn't speak to one another for various financial reasons having to do with Spinney Industries.

Kate sat cross-legged on the floor in only her oxford shirt and underwear, staring vaguely out to sea. She was quiet for a would-be revolutionary. But as her thirtieth birthday approached, she felt an urgent need to discover the Kate side of her as opposed to the Spinney. To break some rules. To defy some conventions. She even had a secret desire to—just once— dance on a table in a bar. Why should Paris Hilton have all the fun?

But so far it remained only a renegade impulse that her brain wouldn't allow her body to follow. Spinneys didn't do such things, unlike Hiltons.

The phone rang and she almost ignored it, but finally got up to see who it was. She didn't get many calls these days, since she hadn't given many people her Florida number.

It was a 617 area code, not surprising, and it was— her heart sank—her unpleasant cousin, Wendell Spinney IV. The last time she'd seen him, he'd made fun of her hair, insulted her and then voted not to allocate funds for a Spinney donation to the Special Olympics.

What did he want? She thought about letting it go to voice mail, but she'd only have to call him back.

"Hello?"

"Katydid. It's Wendell."

She loathed the nickname. "No, Katy didn't. What's up, Wendell? Need a good stock tip?"

"I'm doing pretty well on my own, thanks. But I'm headed down to Miami and I need a place to stay."

"Why are you coming down here?"

"Business," he said vaguely. "Now, about accommodations—"

"That's easy—the Mandarin Oriental."

"I'm not paying those prices." Wendell loved status goods but was incredibly cheap when it came to anything else.

"How about a Motel 6, then?"

"I don't think so."

"Go to the Spinney compound in Palm Beach. You'll be a lot more comfortable there than in my condo. And there's a chef."

"Alistair is there with Lisa and the kids. And don't tell me to just avoid him. It's not possible with those brats."

She sighed. Just when she'd found some peace…

"C'mon, Katy. Where's your sense of family? Besides, I need someone to show me around town."

"Wendell, I'm the wrong person to show you around. I do absolutely nothing but work." Miami was an intimidating town to explore by herself, and she didn't seem to possess the easy familiarity that made other students quick friends.

A brief hope flickered in her: maybe Wendell had become a nice person in the few months since she'd last seen him? Doubtful. Kate grimaced. And she certainly couldn't dance on a table with *him* in the picture.

"I'll be there from the sixth to the tenth," he said. "Can you pick me up at the airport? And Katy, you *do* have a guestroom there?"

"Yes," she admitted reluctantly. "But no bed."

"You get a bed. I'll bring my own sheets."

"Get a bed? Just for you?"

"What's the matter, Katy? Can't afford it?" Sarcasm dripped from his voice. "You need one anyway."

*That's debatable.* But she said, "E-mail me your flight info." Great. It looked like she'd have Wendell's pudgy, pompous ass here whether she wanted it or not. It never ceased to amaze her how he didn't blink at going where he wasn't wanted.

Kate didn't want *any* of her family down here, but she especially didn't wish to see Wendell. However, she felt a certain sense of obligation and kinship—his nuclear family was just as screwed up as her own. Their mothers had been identical twins, down to their matching drug habits. The only difference was that Kate's mother was hooked on barbiturates and Wendell's had been hooked on cocaine. A martini too many on top of it all had stopped her heart when Wendell was three.

"See you soon, Katy," he said into her ear. "Au revoir."

She hung up the phone. Why had she answered it? *Get a bed.* The nerve of the guy! Kate scooted on her butt over to her laptop, which lay on the floor since she still had no furniture in her living room, either.

She logged onto the Internet, found the Web site of a well-known outdoor equipment manufacturer, and zeroed in on what she was looking for. Kate grinned evilly. She'd get a bed for Wendell, all right. One of the blow-up variety. He'd be right at home on the big air bag.

When her order was complete, Kate wandered out onto the balcony and let the wind blow through her hair, inhaling the damp, salty scent. The air here in Miami was thick with humidity, very different from the crisp, briny Cape Cod breeze.

Below her she saw people sunning by the pool, sailboats and yachts out in the ocean; the occasional fishing boat. She'd started to relax and just people-watch when she heard the phone ring again. Tension coiled in her neck and shoulders as she stepped through the door and picked it up. "Wendell, what do you want now?"

"Who is Wendell?" said a deep, amused male voice with a slight South American accent. "Your boyfriend?" The timbre vibrated right down her spine and coiled into her stomach.

"Who's calling?" she asked, even though she recognized the voice immediately. A shimmer of unwilling excitement went through her. She shook it off.

"Alejandro, from the MBA program."

"How did you get my number?"

"From the student roster, Kate. How are you?"

"Uh, fine." A pause ensued, and she tried to remember her manners. "How are you?"

"Fine." The tremor of laughter still echoed in his voice. "So who is Wendell?"

She dragged her bare toe across the sheen of the hardwood floor, leaving a streak. "He's my cousin. My obnoxious cousin, who's invited himself to stay, even though I hinted that he should call a hotel."

"I see," said Alejandro. "Well, maybe you should take pity on him. He's probably saving money for new shoes, too."

Kate snorted. "No need. Not only could Wendell dress in suits made of hundred dollar bills, but he's the type of person who actually travels with shoe trees and polish. So his footwear tends to last longer than mine."

"Ugh. I dislike him immediately," Alejandro said. "But at least I don't have to kill him, now."

"Excuse me?"

"Because he's not your boyfriend."

Kate didn't know how to respond. "You're flirting again," she accused him, suspicious.

"It's a genetic flaw," he told her. "I am unable to help myself."

"I'm so sorry to hear that. But you can kill Wendell if you want to. He's very annoying."

Alejandro laughed, and she loved the sound of it, rich and deep like flavored chocolate. "Kate, *mi corazon,* if he's so bad then why are you letting him stay with you?"

"He's family," she said gloomily.

"Enough said. How long will he be there?"

"Five days. Unless I can persuade him to leave sooner. I'm hoping the blow-up bed will do the trick."

"A blow-up bed won't get rid of anyone with determination. You'll have to make things more uncomfortable than that."

"I'd love to, but I'm not sure how. You can't stick nails into an air mattress."

"Hmm." Alejandro thought for a moment. "Is this Wendell an animal person?"

"No. Not at all. Why?"

"Because I have a friend who could loan you a pot-bellied pig."

Kate choked on a laugh. "A *pig?* You're kidding, right?"

"No, I'm not. And does this Wendell smoke?"

"God, no. He's rabidly anti-nicotine and germ-phobic. The guy travels with his own sheets."

"Then you need a smooth-talking Peruvian to puff cigars in your living room, too."

"Are you trying to invite yourself over?"

"The Yankee catches on."

Kate thought about it, and then said cautiously, "I actually like the smell of cigars, as long as they're good ones."

"And I will bring a large dish of *cau-cau,* which your cousin will be forced to try out of politeness."

"What's *cau-cau?*"

"Tripe. The stomach lining of a cow. It makes most gringos gag, and my Tia Carlotta loves to cook it."

Kate shivered. "That will send dear Wendell right over the edge."

"So when am I coming to dinner? I'm inviting myself for purely altruistic motives," he reassured her. "Only in order to save you, you see."

"Yeah. I am touched by your selflessness, Al."

"No, please not Al. You may call me Alejo, though."

"Alejo," she repeated, liking the exotic sound of it.

"Yes. *Perfecto*. Now, Alejo is coming to dinner on what evening, *mi corazon?*"

"You are shameless," she told him.

*"Sí."* His tone remained warm and amused.

She decided to relent. "I can't believe I'm doing this, but it's for a good cause—Wendell-fumigation. You can come to dinner on Saturday, okay?"

"I am there. *Gracias.*"

"And you'll bring the cigars and the…that nasty stuff."

"Well, as a Peruvian, I don't think it's nasty, but *sí.* You wish me to bring the pot-bellied pig?"

Kate almost said no. Then she looked around. Spinneys didn't bring the barn into the parlor…but Just Kate might. What the hell. She had no carpet for it to soil. And it might be very entertaining to see Wendell's reaction to it. A woman who danced on tables might have a pig in her condo, right?

"I *really* can't believe I'm doing this. But yes. I'll need the pot-bellied pig on the sixth, the night he arrives. It doesn't bite or anything, does it?"

"Not usually. It does squeal, though. And it makes other strange pig noises."

"What does it eat?"

"Purina Mini Pig Chow, of course."

"Of course. Silly me, I should have known that." Purina made *pig* chow? "Is this animal house-trained? Do I take it for walks?"

"Exactly. It's just like a dog with a snout and a curly, non-waggable tail. It even fetches. So, Kate, does this mean we're going to work together on the marketing class project?"

"Is that why you're helping me get rid of my cousin?"

"Maybe."

"We don't even know what the project is yet," she said. Why did he want to work with her so much? What was his agenda? Her money? Her mouth twisted.

"We know that it's a hands-on project, and that we'll be working in teams. He'll tell us the rest next week."

Hands-on. Did Alejandro, self-proclaimed genetic flirt, want to get his hands on her? The thought sent a flash of heat through her body. She'd never had a Latin Lover. The term cracked her up. It sounded so purple, so over the top.

"So what do you say, Kate? Will you trade a partnership for a pot-bellied pig, a cigar and some tripe?"

"Limited liability partnership," she said, hugely entertained. "And I need it in writing that the pig won't bite."

He chuckled. "I can't possibly put that in writing. There's no guarantee with animals. But I'll throw in a roll of duct tape and we have a deal. What you do with it and the pig is your concern. Okay?"

"Okay."

Kate peered over the railing at three buns-up bathing beauties who were abundantly endowed and wore nothing but neon thongs. "Alejandro, you've got to explain something to me. The women down here in Miami—how can they walk around wearing nothing except butt-floss? It's indecent!"

"Butt…*floss,* did you say?"

"Yes. These women down by the pool—they'd get arrested for indecent exposure in Boston."

"Why?"

"Their br—bodacious ta-tas are hanging out! Among other things."

"Kate, they're just breasts and buttocks."

"Yeah, I *noticed.* Where I come from, we cover those things up. We don't display them to the entire United States and all of South America, too."

"What a shame. You're such a Yankee, *mi amorcito.* Women are beautiful. Why not appreciate them?"

"I'm not your little love-morsel, you flirt. And it's fine for women to be attractive, but I think they can be that way without baring their cracks to the planet."

He laughed softly.

"And the flashy men! What's with all the Rolexes and gold bracelets and rings? Talk about conspicuous consumption."

"You're not in Boston anymore, Dorothy. It's just a different style here. Casual but elegant."

*Don't you mean tacky?*

"You will get used to Miami soon. And," he said provocatively, "I think you'd look wonderful in a thong yourself."

"You couldn't get me into one of those if I were *dead,* sport." She shuddered. "And people wonder why there are shark attacks in Florida?"

She watched, scandalized, as one of the bathing beauties sat up, rubbed oil shamelessly all over her bare gazangas, and then lay back down tits-up. Unbelievable.

"When in Rome, Kate."

"At least in Rome they wore togas!"

"Yes, before and after the orgies."

"Orgies? How did we get onto this topic, Alejandro?"

"I believe you asked me how Miami women can wear thongs. It's because they're not uptight like Yankees."

"I am *not* uptight."

"Describe your own bathing suit, then."

"It's a navy blue one-piece."

He chortled. "That says it all, Kate."

She felt like growling. "Well, if I'm so uptight, then why do you want to work with me? Why are you riding to my rescue with a pot-bellied pig?"

A long pause ensued. Finally he said, "Because I think you're bright and beautiful and in a class by yourself." All traces of teasing were gone from his voice.

Kate's knees wobbled, and she sat down abruptly on the rough cement of her balcony. Tears pricked at the back of her eyes. "Who paid you to say that?"

"Nobody paid me, *tesorito*. What's the matter, you can't take a compliment?"

A lump formed in her throat and she knew she needed to get off the phone before she embarrassed herself. "I can accept a compliment," she insisted. "But I'm thinking you need an eye exam, since you're a little young for cataracts. I've got to go, Alejandro. See you in class Monday."

"Oh, very flattering. I say something nice, and I'm told I need an eye appointment. I suppose I need a cane and some Viagra, as well?"

"You tell me," she said, before she could stop herself.

"I'd be more than happy to show you that I don't."

Kate experienced a flash of heat, but she just laughed.

He cleared his throat. "It's been a pleasure talking with you, my stiff-necked little Yankee. Enjoy your weekend."

"You, too." Suddenly she didn't want to end the conversation, but she'd already given the signal. She wondered what gorgeous, strapping Latin men did on weekends in Miami, then looked down at the row of juicy bottoms in their thongs again and decided she didn't want to know.

Despite her Harvard degree, Alejandro had the last word. "And Kate? While I maintain that I don't need Viagra, you *definitely* need new shoes."

## 4

KATE STARED AT the forty-seven-pound miniature pot-bellied pig outside her building's freight elevator. It stared right back with a porky little grin.

"Meet Gracious," said Alejandro, who had her on a leash just like a dog.

Kate was torn between helplessly admiring his biceps and chest in the tight, black T-shirt he wore, and fascination with the animal. The men she knew wore loose golf attire or heavy, cable-knit wool sweaters. They didn't look as if they'd stepped off the set of *Miami Vice*. And if they had anything on a leash, it was more likely to be a springer spaniel or a golden retriever, not Vietnamese livestock.

Alejandro was perfectly proportioned, like a classical statue out of a coffee table art book. His torso stretched in a triangle from wide shoulders down to a trim waist over long, lean legs. Snug denim covered those. The black T-shirt was tucked into the jeans, he wore no belt, and on his feet were black European-style slip-on shoes of high-quality leather. The only other accessory he wore was that killer white smile of his. Oh, and the dreadful gold chain around his neck—but she decided to ignore that.

"Gracious," he said as they rode up to her floor in the elevator, "likes raisins, dried fruit, grapes, melon and veggies. Her favorite thing in the world is dried apricots."

Gracious was black with light brown eyes and fuzzier than Kate had expected, though the fuzz was wiry and her skin was visible in places. She had pink discolorations on her snout that looked like big freckles. Kate swallowed as the pig cocked her head at her and came forward to sniff at her ankles. She made a grunting noise and looked up at Kate with surprising intelligence. The animal was quite cute in a homely way.

"How did you, er, meet Gracious?" Kate asked, starting to regret her impulsive decision to board the pig while Cousin Wendell mooched her guest room.

"She belongs to my next-door neighbor, and periodically she gets under the fence and hangs out in my yard."

"And your neighbor is okay with loaning her out?"

"He's an artist with a great sense of humor. I told him that Gracious was needed for a family pest-control situation." Alejandro grinned.

They exited the elevator and walked to her apartment, where she unlocked the door and held it open. "You're sure that Gracious is house-trained?"

"Positive. She even has a litter box. She'll also go outdoors, though. She's happier outside during the day, but unless she has her baby pool it's just too hot right now."

"Baby pool?"

He nodded. "Pigs don't sweat, and they overheat very easily. So my neighbor always has one of those kiddie pools going for her. You'll need to take her for regular walks, twice a day minimum."

"Wendell will just love this." Kate smirked.

Alejandro handed her the pig's leash while he hauled a bag of food and a large plastic under-bed storage container into her condo. "I'll have to go back down for the litter. I left it in the car." He took a moment to look around. "Nice place, Kate. But what do you sit on?"

"The floor. I'll get around to furniture one of these days."

"Where do you study? Do you pull a chair up to the stove?"

"I read and work on my laptop in bed."

His eyes gleamed, and suddenly she had an image of his lean, muscular body and smooth brown skin against her cool white sheets. The moisture disappeared from her mouth; it felt filled with sand.

She rejected the image. She was here in Miami to get an MBA and figure out who Just Kate was, not to party naked with a dangerously attractive, highly unsuitable Peruvian man. She didn't want to lose her identity to some guy before she even had a handle on it herself. Especially not a guy who was so smooth that he could probably talk her clothes into flying off her body by themselves.

Kate frowned and changed the subject, before she could reflect that partying naked with Alejandro could fit in quite nicely with that revolution she was planning—and might even lead straight to the table she wanted to dance on.

"Gracious is probably here illegally. I doubt the zoning in this building allows livestock, so I'll use the freight elevator when I take her out and just hope nobody sees me."

Alejandro nodded. "I have a bag of toys for her. If she doesn't have toys to play with, she'll root, meaning you could find tiles or molding pried up."

While he went to get the toys, the pig walked over to the window and stood looking out at the view. She sat down on her haunches.

Kate eyed her and went to the refrigerator to see if she had any acceptable piggy cuisine. Alejandro had said something about grapes, hadn't he? She pulled out a bowl of seedless purple grapes and plucked a couple off the stem. Then she walked back into the living room and sat down a few feet from the animal.

"Look what I have, Miss Piggy. Would you like one?"

Gracious trotted over immediately and snuffled the grape out of her palm. She made happy little porcine noises as she consumed it, and Kate laughed. She scratched the pig's head, surprised that she didn't smell bad at all.

They'd made friends by the time Alejandro got back—the pig sat leaning into Kate's thigh, her eyes closed as she savored having her ears rubbed.

"She'll sleep with you if you let her," he said. The gleam shot back into his eyes, as if to say that he would, too. "But if you don't want her on your bed, you can just fold up a blanket on the floor for her." He walked to the sliding glass door and looked out at Biscayne Bay.

"You have an amazing view."

While he looked out at the water, she couldn't help looking up at him. Up the length of those long, masculine legs to the certifiably fine ass and the casual cock of his hips. He was so close that she could smell the detergent he used to wash his jeans and the leather of his shoes. She caught a whiff of breezy aftershave, too.

Gracious seemed to understand and empathize with her appreciation of the man. She emitted a little squeal. Kate got up to get her another couple of grapes, and felt small next to Alejandro. He turned his head and looked down at her, his eyes black, enigmatic and beyond the outer boundaries of sexy. The adjective that leaped to mind was *compelling*.

If she didn't look away from those eyes she was going to do something stupid. So she dropped her gaze to his chest again, the defined contours of muscle clearly visible under the black cotton. "Kate," he said softly.

She leaped away, fixating on the first thing she saw, the shallow plastic box for the pig's litter. "So what do you use to line this with?"

"A large trash bag." He'd dropped some into the sack of litter, and now he pulled one out and shook it open for her.

"I can't believe I'm resorting to these measures to get rid of my cousin," she babbled.

He shrugged. "It does seem a little out of character. I mean, you had no problem telling Kurtz he was wrong. So why can't you tell this cousin to go somewhere else?"

She picked at her ragged cuticles.

He watched her, seemed about to say something, and then looked away and shut his mouth.

"I don't know. This is different. Wendell is a pain in

the ass, but…he doesn't really have anyone else. And he's family."

"You've hinted that you came down here to get away from your family."

"Yes. Sometimes it's harder than you might think."

"You are close to them?"

She expelled a breath. "Close? I'm not sure how to answer that. We certainly fight a lot. We see each other a few times a year, since most of us have seats on the board, and everyone's scheming and maneuvering to get their particular interests and projects green-lighted. So there are alliances…" She stopped. *You're talking too much, Kate.* "It's not exactly the *Brady Bunch.*"

Gracious started to turn circles and dig at the molding in a corner of the living room. "What is she doing?"

"Do you need to go out, little one?" Alejandro asked. He picked up the end of the leash and looked at Kate, tongue in cheek. "*Señorita,* would you care for a romantic stroll on the beach with Miss Piggy?"

"Sure, I'll tag along." Kate sent him a sidelong glance. "But you might want to liquor her up before you make any smooth moves on her."

He raised an eyebrow and glanced sharply at her. "What are you implying, Kate?"

"Nothing."

"I'll have you know that my intentions—at least regarding Gracious—are purely honorable."

ALEJANDRO THOUGHT KATE looked even more beautiful in knee-length, baggy khaki shorts—they were awful, but at least he could see her long, slim legs—with her hair flying around her face in the wind.

Gracious had a difficult time on the beach with her short little legs sinking into the sand, but she was able to sample various aperitifs: seaweed, driftwood, even a rotting fish. So she was happy enough.

They got some odd looks regarding the pig, but other than a couple of kids who ran up to pet her, nobody bothered them.

Alejo wanted to bother Kate, however, in the worst way. He wanted to kiss each of those arrogant cheekbones, taste her smart Yankee mouth, steal her breath away. But he did none of those things, contenting himself with teasing her and savoring the way she looked all wild and free and windblown.

"I see that you went to the most exclusive grocery store aisle for your new shoes, Kate." He gestured to the rubber flip-flops on her feet.

"Yeah, I saved up and had them custom-made," she said dryly. "Like them?"

"They're gorgeous." If ever a woman was in dire need of a pedicure and a manicure, it was Kate Spinney. But to say so crossed the line between teasing and just plain rude.

"They bring my total for shoes up to six pairs—the loafers, some cross-trainers, snow boots, ski boots and one pair of serviceable black pumps."

"You're kidding me, right?"

She shook her head.

"My last girlfriend had one-hundred and forty-six pairs of shoes."

Kate goggled at him. "Was her name Imelda? What does any human being do with that many shoes?"

Actually, she'd liked to wear a lot of them in the bedroom, but he didn't think it was a good idea to mention that. Alejandro shrugged. "She was very stylish."

Kate shoved her hands into the pockets of her wrinkled shorts and grimaced. "Oh. How nice for her. And you, I guess."

He liked the fact that the topic of his ex-girlfriend obviously irritated her. But he also took his cue. "She wasn't nearly as beautiful as you are."

Kate snorted, sounding very much like Gracious. In fact, the pig's head came up and she looked around for other porcine companions. Disappointed, she went back to rooting in the sand.

"Do they teach you to do that at Harvard?" Alejandro asked, grinning.

"Yeah. We take Barnyard Noises 101 our first semester. Didn't you know that? It's part of the language requirement. You probably took something useless like French."

"Spanish. I knew a lot from my mother, but I needed the grammar and the spelling."

"Ha." Kate shot him a look. "You needed a blow-off class."

He laughed. "Okay. Guilty as charged."

"Where did you go to school?"

"Right here at Miami."

"Wasn't it hard to study with the beach and the night-life and all?"

He shrugged. "Nah, you get used to it. You start to

take it for granted. I'll admit that Miami is probably not the intellectual capital of the world, but the university is a good one."

"So are you from a big family?"

"No. Not here. I do have extended family in Peru. But growing up, it was just me and my mother and Tia Carlotta, her friend."

"Friend or *friend?*"

Alejandro stopped and looked down at her. "Kate, are you asking me whether my mother was a lesbian?" He dissolved into laughter.

"What?" she said. "So what if I was?"

"It's just that she's spinning in her grave right now," he gasped. "And Tia Carlotta would grind you up and stuff peppers with you. It's just a rude thing to ask about! What's *your* mother's sexual orientation?"

"Sorry," she muttered. "I guess I am pretty…direct. As for my mother, I don't think she really has a sexual orientation. She just plays a lot of golf, and she's heavily involved with the symphony."

Gracious was pulling them ever closer to the water, leaving little hoof tracks in the wet sand. Alejandro tugged her back a little, and she tried to be clever and bypass him by going around Kate. The result was a tangle, with Kate somehow snugged up against his chest.

To be honest, he could have solved the problem quite easily. But he could smell the sweet citrus scent of her hair as it blew across his chin, and his arm seemed to fit perfectly around her, and then she looked up at him with those wary green eyes. "Alejandro?"

He really couldn't help it. He bent his head and

kissed her, tasting and parting her lips—those lips that were way too soft for the words that came out of them.

She went rigid for a moment, and then relaxed in his arms and melted into him with a sigh.

He brought his free hand up and cupped her jaw, tangled his hand in her hair and kissed her even more deeply, exploring her mouth with his tongue, touching hers, stroking. Kate made an incoherent sound and backed away, only to catch the heel of her flip-flop in the sand and fall over Gracious.

Their tender moment ended in an explosive squeal, flying sand and an undignified shriek. So much for romance.

He was Mr. Smooth. But as Alejandro helped Kate up, dusted her off, calmed the pig and steered all of them back to the stretch of sand outside her condo, he knew one thing: he definitely wanted to keep kissing this woman. He wanted to kiss her in much steamier places, and without anything baggy and ugly obscuring her body.

"Don't do that again," Kate said, avoiding his gaze.

"Why not? You liked it."

"Because I'm not sure *why* you did it."

"I did it because I liked it, too."

"Is that the only reason?"

He stared at her, half amused and half annoyed. What, did she think he was after her money?

Her hair flew out around her face in all directions, courtesy of the wind. With her thin frame, she looked like a suspicious Yankee dandelion. "Should there be another reason?"

Kate avoided the question with yet another one. "Besides, how do you know I liked it? I might have been faking it, melting into your arms just so I could yank off your nuts."

*"Dios mio!"* Alejandro dropped the pig's leash and took Kate by the shoulders, while she looked up at him with mingled fear, belligerence and hope. Then he dropped his mouth to hers again. "You, *mi vida,* are a head case."

He parted her stubborn mouth with his and slid inside, finding sweetness where she pretended only vinegar lived. He found her sharp tongue and sucked it until it softened and mated with his. He could taste her reluctance but also a growing excitement, a core of wildness that he wanted to split open and savor.

When he raised his head, he played to that wildness. "You know where I'm going to do that next, *mi amorcito?* Hmm?"

She gazed up at him and shook her head.

"Between your legs."

Grinning, he caught the hand that came up to smack him and wrapped it around the pig's leash instead. "Good night, Kate. See you in class."

She appeared to have lost her voice. When she found it again she yelled after him, "I'll see you in *hell,* sport."

He turned and grinned at her as he walked away into the night. "Great. I hear they have plenty of beds there."

# 5

THE LATIN LOVER had kissed her. Kate still couldn't quite believe it. Or rather, she could believe he'd done it, but not that she'd let him. She lectured herself sternly.

*He's a hound. He'd seduce anything in a skirt, and he's just after you because of the Spinney money and the challenge. Remember, he said that flirting is a genetic trait in him—he can't help it. So what are you doing, letting him stick his tongue into your mouth? What are you doing, allowing him to talk to you that way?*

But his dirty words had given her a dirty thrill. Heat, moisture and electricity had flashed to the very place he'd said he wanted to kiss next. And they flashed there again as she thought about him.

She poured a little Purina Mini Pig Chow into a bowl for Gracious, amused that the pig started drooling and making noise as soon as she saw the bag. Then her amusement vanished.

*Is that what I'm doing? Drooling and squealing over Alejandro Torres? Well, that's disgusting.*

Still, the guy could kiss. And his chest! She could tell, even through the T-shirt, that his torso rippled with muscle. Was his family business a chain of gyms? Did he work on engines all day? No—no grease under the nails. In fact, they were immaculate. But whatever Alejandro did, it was very male-oriented.

Kate found herself wondering just what he looked like without his shirt. Then she wondered what it would be like to kiss him without his shirt, be captive against that solid, hard chest. And finally she dispensed with his pants, too—who needed those, after all?

Alejandro strutted stark naked through her mind, and then turned around and strutted back. He winked at her. Kate turned down the air-conditioning, since the temperature seemed to be rising in the condo.

The problem was that however outrageous, the man made her feel things, made her feel alive. Shocks had rushed through her as soon as he touched her lips, threaded his fingers into her hair, hauled her against him. She'd almost liquefied.

Spinneys didn't liquefy. She was certain of it. None of those prune-faced people peering out from the gilt frames in her parents' formal living room had ever had a sexual urge: impossible. Spinneys didn't make love; they bred the next generation.

Spinneys especially didn't hook up with very tan, muscular hunks o' burnin' love who could model tighty whities on a billboard or star in a Bowflex commercial. But…maybe Just Kate did. And hadn't Maria Shriver married Arnold Schwarzenegger?

Hadn't Kate come down here to Miami to escape being a Spinney? Break out of the preppy WASP mold? Wasn't her goal to shake her booty on that table and have a good time?

Yes, it was.

So where did that leave her as far as twining tongues with Mr. Latin Lover? He'd probably helped dozens of women dance on tables. So maybe she shouldn't act so predictably, Waspishly outraged at his words. Maybe she should hold him to his dirty promise, and use him for her own ends. Maybe Just Kate had a new boy toy, and the power could be all hers. She just had to figure out how to take it.

THE FLUORESCENT LIGHTING in the auditorium flickered and vibrated, hurting Alejandro's eyes and annoying him. Thank God there were only fifteen minutes left of marketing and then they only had to get through the last class of the day: stats.

He'd come in a couple of minutes late as usual, earning a glare from Kurtz. And Kate hadn't saved him a seat—stupid to be disappointed, since she'd tried to slap him for what he'd said to her, but he was. So he sat in the back row in case he fell asleep.

"Now for your semester projects," Kurtz announced. "They will be worth fifty percent of your grade, so be thorough. I want you to work in pairs, and each pair will identify a business in the Miami area that you feel could benefit from a marketing analysis, new direction and plan. You will complete the analysis, come up with that new direction and forge a business plan that supports and executes the new approach. It's a bonus if you can get the business to actually implement it, but of course I won't grade you on that aspect. Any questions?"

Kurtz clarified a few things that students had

concerns about. Alejandro wondered if Spinney Industries had a Miami office he and Kate could study. Or there was always Benito's, the restaurant around the corner from After Hours. Benny hadn't been doing so well lately, since a bottle of chianti had fallen on a customer's head and given the guy a concussion. Benito was worried about a lawsuit, and his concerns had affected his cooking.

Alejo waylaid Kate as she exited the auditorium. "Hello, *mi amorcito*."

"Well if it isn't the Latin Lover," she said with a smirk.

Interesting. He'd been expecting the silent treatment. "No, no. You can't call me that. It's far too generic. I'm unique. You wouldn't just kiss any Latin Lover, would you, Kate?"

"Lower your voice," she snapped, looking around to see if anyone had heard. She was so repressed it made him smile. He pushed her even harder.

"You're embarrassed to kiss me? Why is that? Are you afraid that once we sleep together, I'll wave your panties around like a flag? I won't, you know."

"Aren't you presuming a hell of a lot, sport?" Her cheekbones flashed at him and her eyes glinted dangerously.

He looked into her eyes for a long moment and watched her color rise adorably. "No," he said simply.

She flushed scarlet. "Wrong answer."

"You're sure about that?"

Kate didn't reply. A pulse beat, wild and irregular, in her throat. It told him all he needed to know.

"So, about the project. We are still teaming up, aren't

we? Or are you welshing on our deal, concerned about your self-control around me?"

Her mouth opened, and then she shut it with a snap. "Listen here, sport. I don't welsh on deals and I don't have *any* issues with self-control. Got that?"

He nodded. Did she call everyone *sport* when she was angry at them? It was vile. "So why don't we both think of a few businesses over the next couple of days and get back in touch?"

"Why don't we just meet tomorrow?"

*Because I'll be fondling ladies' feet all day.* "I work tomorrow."

"What is it that you do, again?"

"Accounting," he lied. It was sort of true. He did keep the books for the business.

"Can't you meet for lunch? It's nowhere near tax season," she pointed out.

He shook his head with regret. "I have a client whose books are in bad shape." *Yeah, if Peggy doesn't start balancing the checkbook when she orders supplies, I'm going to wring her little red-headed neck.* Again, it wasn't a total lie....

"Well, okay. I guess we can talk about it when you come for the delicious tripe dinner with Wendell on Saturday," she said. "And now that I know your true colors, I won't even feel bad about inflicting him on you. You deserve him."

IT WAS A sad fact of life that Wendell Spinney IV, Kate's cousin, looked much more like a pig than, well, a pig. Wendell had been born with sparse blond hair, a wide, moon-shaped face, florid skin and a nose that had an unfortunate tendency to turn up at the end. While he didn't snort, per se, he wore a permanently disgruntled expression that made him look as if he were about to do so.

Kate stared ahead impassively as they walked from her car to her residential building. Like most of the high-rises in Miami, it was tall, sleek and white. Glass doors protected the entrance and inside was a veritable jungle of tropical plants and a small fountain, as well as a modern concierge desk well-manned by helpful staff.

Her cousin swept his muddy-blond hair off his forehead and complained for the seventeenth time about the humidity. "Tell me again why you decided to move to Hell's Sweaty Armpit?" he asked, the damp circles under his own arms growing.

"Business school," she reminded him.

"And what's wrong with Wharton?"

She sighed. "Everybody we know goes to Wharton."

"So? That's a good thing. And it's still in *America*. You don't have to learn Spanish up there."

"Careful, Wendell—your flabby racist underbelly is showing. I happen to like Miami, humidity and all, so if you want to stay in my condo, you'd best watch your mouth."

He curled his lip. "And if you want my votes for your muscular dystrophy charity then you'll watch yours."

She'd forgotten how loathsome Wendell could be, but apparently she was going to remember over the next five days. Goody. They stepped into the elevator and she punched the correct button. They rode up in silence.

The elevator opened at her floor, and they got off, Wendell rolling his suitcase behind him. They arrived at her door and she opened it, ushering her cousin inside.

Immediately he went to the sliding glass doors and took in the view. "Not bad," he said. "What did you pay for this place?"

Typical Wendell. Before she could answer, the clatter of mini-pig hooves on the hardwood floors had him turning around. "Katy, what in the—" His jaw went slack at the sight of the porcine visitor.

"Wendell, this is Gracious. She's staying with me for a few days, while her owner is out of town."

"The hell she is! *I'm* staying with you for a few days."

"So is she."

Wendell squinted at the pig in disbelief. "I'm not living with a barnyard animal."

Gracious grunted at him, backed up, sat down and squealed, laying her ears back. Then she looked up at Kate, clearly echoing Wendell's sentiments. Kate translated the squeal to mean, "I'm not hanging out with that fat, preppy cretin."

"You're both going to have to deal with one another," she said, her lips twitching.

Gracious heaved herself to her feet and waddled over to sniff out Wendell's suitcase. She nudged it with her snout and knocked it over.

"Hey!"

She laid her ears back and cocked her head at him. Then she started snuffling around the zipper.

"Get away from there!" Wendell ran forward, waving his arms, but didn't have the desired effect. Gracious snorted, squealed and redirected her energies: she charged him.

Wendell changed directions on a dime and fled in the other direction, but the pig was fast—who knew?—and pursued him into the kitchen, knocking against his calf with her snout. Wendell leaped for the counter and hauled himself up onto it belly first, his legs flailing. "Kate, do something!"

Gracious appeared very pleased by his response. Kate could have sworn she was grinning. She squealed and then snorted for punctuation.

"You threatened her, Wendell. For all intents and purposes, you charged her first. She was just standing up for herself."

"Lock her up!" he yelled.

"Gracious, come here." Kate tugged gently on the pig's collar, and after a couple of tries got her to follow her into the bathroom. "Look, sweetie, there's a nice fuzzy rug to lie on, okay? I'll get you an apricot. Don't let the mean man hurt your feelings."

"Mean man?" Wendell hollered. "For God's sake, Katy! Do you have a goat in the bedroom? Chickens in the pantry?"

Kate shut the door on Gracious and went back to the kitchen, hands on her hips. "Wendell, you can come down now. Let me show you to your room."

He slid off the granite countertop and onto the floor with a grunt. Then he stalked to his suitcase, wiped imaginary specks of pig drool off the zipper, and towed it after him to the guestroom, where he eyed the air mattress with even more outrage. "You can't expect me to sleep on that! I told you to get a bed."

"That is a bed."

"No, that's a rectangular balloon."

"Wendell, this room is going to be my office and I don't want it filled with a huge guest bed that will hardly ever be used. It's going to be occupied by a desk and a chair and a filing cabinet."

"You said you would get a bed." His tone was belligerent.

Kate looked heavenward. "Take it or leave it. If it bothers you so much, I can make you a reservation somewhere."

Wendell grumbled a bit more and partially unpacked his suitcase into the room's closet, pointing out that she had no chest of drawers, either. Then he requested a cappuccino.

She didn't own an espresso machine. Totally demoralized, her cousin allowed her to take him to the News Café on South Beach, a spot even Kate knew about. It was a gorgeous morning, with few clouds in the sky. They parked on Collins Avenue and walked the few blocks to Ocean Drive. Wendell had plenty to occupy him in making fun of the tourists.

"Check out that hideous Hawaiian shirt, Katy," he said with a smirk. She ignored him, because sitting right there at one of the little café tables was none other than Alejandro Torres, with not one but *two* beautiful women. So that's what good-looking Latin men did on the weekends in Miami.

"Kate?" he called. "Kate, is that you?"

Wendell nudged her. "Hey, Romeo over there with the gold chain around his neck is trying to get your attention."

Kate's gaze honed in on Alejandro's neck and repressed a shudder, as usual. There were just certain unwritten laws. Men in her social circles didn't wear gold chains, and they didn't wear bracelets or diamond pinky rings. A discreet gold watch on a leather band and perhaps a very plain wedding ring—that was all the jewelry a gentleman wore, besides elegant cuff links when the occasion demanded it.

"Who is that guy?" Wendell asked her. "How do you know him?" His lip curled. "He looks like Eric Estrada."

"He does not! And he's in my business school class," Kate told him, liking her cousin's attitude even less than the gold chain. "He's very nice." *And he's a fantastic kisser.* "Actually, he's coming to dinner on Saturday, because we're working on a project for marketing together. You get to try Peruvian food."

Wendell clutched his stomach and rolled his eyes.

"Don't be an ass," Kate told him. "Broaden your cultural horizons. Now make nice."

# 6

ALEJANDRO WATCHED KATE approach with a man who looked remarkably like Gracious, but with a less pleasant expression. Smugness poured out of his pockets and he seemed very impressed with himself.

"Is that *the* Kate?" Peggy elbowed him. Marly looked just as curious as she did.

"That is *the* Kate," Alejandro said, his eyes riveted to her pale, chiseled lips. Lips that he wanted to kiss again. She walked easily, loose-limbed and unselfconscious and sexy because of it. Most of the south Florida women were very aware of their looks and the power they had over men. Not Kate. She didn't wear a smudge of makeup, her hair was an unruly mess, and she looked rumpled, as if she'd just rolled out of bed. It turned him on unbelievably.

He shot Peg and Marly a sidelong glance. "I will skin both of you alive if you give away my secret, do you understand? The Spinney Industries heiress isn't going to date a manicurist."

"She's pretty," Peg said.

"But not at all what I expected," Marly finished for her. They fell silent as *the* Kate approached.

"Hi, Alejandro," Kate said as they got to his table. "Nice to see you. May I introduce my cousin, Wendell Spinney?"

"The fourth," Wendell added.

"Right," Kate said, deadpan. "The fourth."

Alejandro raised an eyebrow. "Must be very confusing, all those Wendell Spinneys walking around and bumping into one another." He smiled. "I'm Alejandro Torres—the first."

Kate fought with a smile.

"And these are my friends and clients, Peggy Underwood and Marly Fine. Peggy, Marly, meet Kate Spinney and Wendell…the fourth."

Kate's eyes went to Peg and Marly. She seemed a little intimidated by Marly's looks, but then, a lot of women were. Marly, with her long dark hair and spectacular blue-green eyes, was gorgeous. But she smiled and stuck out her foot. "Look, Kate, we have the same flip-flops."

Kate grinned. "Big bucks at the Winn-Dixie, right?"

"You got it."

Wendell eyed their rubber thong sandals as if they were cockroaches, and changed the subject. "What sort of business are you in, Al?" He inquired.

"It's Alejandro, or Alejo if you prefer. And I'm an accountant. Peggy and Marly are my clients—they own a salon and spa in Coral Gables."

The two girls looked delighted. "You gonna put that in wri—" Peg began, before Alejo kicked her hard under the table.

"Is that so? Well, speaking of salons, Kate and I have

interests in shampoo, don't we, Kate? Among other things." Wendell's lips stretched into a proprietary smile.

She edged away from him, obviously uncomfortable with the subject of the Spinney holdings, and said nothing.

"Why don't you join us for some coffee?" Peggy suggested. "We can pull up a couple of chairs."

"Sure," Kate said.

At the same time Wendell said, "Oh, thank you but we're running late." He looked at his watch, a Tiffany that Alejo estimated was white gold and had cost more than the down payment on a large house.

*Pompous ass.* "Oh? Where are you rushing off to?"

"Nowhere," Kate replied.

"We have an appointment," Wendell said in stuffy tones. "Remember, Kate?"

"Wendell does have an appointment, now that I think about it," she exclaimed, green eyes sparkling with malice. "I'd forgotten—you promised to take Gracious to the groomer's for me today, didn't you?"

"Wha—? Bu—"

"Wendell noticed that she had a faint *eau de piggy.*"

"How is Gracious?" Marly asked. "We haven't seen her for a while, Alejo. It was hilarious when he brought her to the spa," she explained to Kate, "because she unerringly went straight to the treatment room where we give the mud baths and all. If the door had been unlocked, I think she would have climbed right in with the customer."

Kate laughed.

"You let a pig into your spa?" Wendell appeared scandalized. "That's highly unsanitary!"

"Why? She's cleaner than the average dog, and customers bring their small dogs in occasionally." Peggy stuck up for Gracious.

"That's abominable, too." Wendell sat down reluctantly in one of the chairs that Alejandro finally brought over, since The Fourth made no move to do so. Kate sat in the other one.

A waitress appeared and asked for their orders.

"Black coffee," Kate requested.

"Skinny half-caf, no-whip, white-chocolate mocha cappuccino with a two shakes of cinnamon and one shake of nutmeg," Wendell told her.

The waitress snapped her gum. "Whad'ya think this is, Starbuckets? Try again, from the menu, pal. There's Mexican coffee, Italian, French, Jamaican, Spanish—"

Wendell's nostrils flared. "Are you aware that you work in a service industry, mademoiselle?"

She rolled her eyes. "Naw, I woke up thinking I was the Queen of England. Now what'll it be?"

"What is your name? And I'd like to speak to the manager."

"Wendell, please. Can we just have a cup of joe and relax?" Kate begged him. "Does everything have to be a production?"

"What kind of establishment is this?" he fumed.

"It's the News Café," Marly said. "Famous."

"I don't see why. We're leaving." And he stood up.

"Wendell, I need to discuss the marketing project

with Alejandro," Kate told him. "Why don't you walk over to Collins Avenue and do some shopping? It's a little like Newberry Street. Or you could take my keys and run Gracious over to the groomer's."

He cast her a look of dislike. "Fine, I'll go to Collins. The barnyard animal can wait."

Just then, the manager on duty approached. "Something wrong, sir?"

"Your staff is rude, your menu lacking and your chairs uncomfortable. Your mugs are thick and ugly, this humidity is wretched—"

"I'm sorry you feel that way, sir."

"Well, what are you going to do about it?"

"Uh…we've served the same coffee in the same cups from the same menu for years, now. And our customers have sat in the same chairs. The weather I can't change for you, and my staff is incapable of bringing you something that is not on the menu."

"Do you know who I *am?*" asked Wendell, puffing up with hot air like a bagpipe.

"No, sir. I do wish we could make you happier. But considering your long list of complaints, I doubt that's possible, so let me show you out…."

Alejandro gave Kate a lot of credit for not laughing until Cousin Wendell was out of earshot. Then they all broke down.

"I didn't know they even *made* relatives that bad," Alejo said in wondering tones. "Kate, tell me the rest of your family isn't like that."

She eyed him gloomily. "They're all either workaholic, comatose, psychopathic or just generally unbearable. Actually my brother's great—but he's gay, so the rest of them don't speak to him. Unbelievable. They treat him as though he's brought more shame on the family than another cousin of mine who'd be a convicted rapist if he hadn't gotten off on a technicality."

"Is he cute?" asked Peggy.

"The rapist?"

"No! Your brother. Because maybe we should set him up with Nicky. He's one of our hairstylists, and he's always going on these disastrous Internet dates."

Alejo kicked her again.

"Ow!" she said, glaring at him.

Kate's nose was in her coffee cup, so she didn't notice. "Yes, my brother is good-looking. Is Nicky?"

Peg looked at Alejandro and Marly. "Yes. But he does have somewhat astonishing taste in clothes."

"Enough about Nicky," Alejandro said. "Let's talk about the marketing project. Do you have any ideas?"

"What's your project?" Marly asked before Kate could answer.

"We have to do an analysis, come up with a new direction and write a marketing plan for a business in the Miami area," she explained.

"Oh, how interesting!" His two partners exchanged a glance. A mischievous glance.

He narrowed his eyes at them.

They looked back, all innocence.

"I think it will be," Kate nodded. "We just have to come up with a business."

Alejandro closed his eyes and initiated a violent coughing fit as Peg and Marly said together, "What about After Hours? Our salon and spa? We could use some marketing analysis and help."

*Noooooo!* "I'm sure Kate is looking for something with a much bigger scope," Alejo broke in. "Something that will really challenge us."

"Actually, I love the idea!" said Kate. "It fits right in with my background of Spinney products."

"Uh. But aren't you bored with that?" Alejandro asked, a bit desperately. "Surely you want to broaden your horizons a little." No way could he have Kate sniffing around the salon! She'd figure out what he was really doing for a living. She'd laugh. She wouldn't respect him. She'd think he was a *rosquete.* He cringed.

Kate frowned at him. "No. I think this is *perfect.* And you already do the accounting for After Hours, right? So you're familiar with the numbers, which is always a good thing. Let's do it!"

Peg and Marly grinned like two Cheshire cats upon discovering a cream factory.

He sent them a murderous look.

They high-fived each other, completely unconcerned.

*Beauty Boy! Beauty Boy!* The old taunt echoed through his head.

The waitress stopped back by now that Wendell was blessedly gone and offered more coffee. *Yes, please. And can you lace mine with cyanide?*

He was going to boil Peggy in her own massage oil, Alejandro thought as he turned his Porsche into Tia Carlotta's driveway. And he would cut off Marly's head with her texturing shears. How could they have done that to him? The last thing he wanted was Kate anywhere near After Hours. She couldn't find out his secret. A woman like her would never date a manicurist.

He shut off the engine and gave the little three-bedroom house a critical once-over. He needed to oil Tia's storm shutters and make sure the drainpipes were clear before hurricane season started up.

Tia Carlotta opened the door before he was even on the porch. "Alejo! *Como estas? Bien?*"

"*Sí, bien, gracias. Y tu?*" He kissed her on the cheek. Tia wore a sky-blue tunic over a black stretchy skirt, her hair pulled straight back from her face. She looked younger than her sixty-two years and credited this in equal parts to piety and Youth Dew.

"Something smells wonderful, Tia," Alejandro told her as he followed her into the house.

"I made you *choritos, escabeche de pescado* and the *cau-cau*," she said.

"You shouldn't have gone to so much trouble."

"It's no trouble, not for my poor Manuela's boy, God rest her soul." Whenever Tia spoke his mother's name, which was often, she asked God to rest her soul. Alejo figured Mama's soul had to be in a coma by now, but of course he was never so disrespectful as to say so.

"So, you take all of this to a dinner party?" she inquired. "Who comes?"

Alejandro shrugged. "Just a couple of friends."

"One of these friends is a girl?"

He nodded, trying his best to look ultra-casual.

"This girl, will I meet her one day?"

He thought about Kate's *gringa,* Yankee manners, and Tia's extreme suspicion when it came to any girl-friend of his. "Maybe," he said cautiously.

Tia Carlotta was perfectly capable of mashing Kate's left breast in a garlic press if she took a dislike to her and got her alone. Then again, Kate was almost certainly capable of fighting back with a meat cleaver.

Alejo shuddered. He wasn't eager for them to get acquainted anytime soon.

"*Maybe,* he says. Maybe I take you by the ear and put you out, eh?"

"Now, Tia," he said soothingly. "Don't take it that way. I only meant that I might not think she's worthy of meeting you."

"I no meet a girlfriend of yours since sixteen years, your prom!"

Alejo shrugged. "When I'm ready to get married, you'll meet her. Until then, why would you want to? I'm not serious about her if I don't bring her to see you."

She sighed in exasperation and handed him a spoon. "You taste," she said, pushing him towards the stove.

The *cau-cau* simmered away on a front burner, happily getting slimier and more rubbery in its rich yellow sauce.

It was the consistency of tripe, the texture that most gringos couldn't stomach. Alejo liked it, since he'd grown up on it. He took a big spoonful and blew gently on it, waiting for it to cool.

She'd done a good job on it, as usual. Tia was a fabulous cook. "*Perfecto,*" he said, making noises of appreciation as he swallowed. "*Esta fabuloso.*"

Tia preened. "Yes? It doesn't need nothing? Salt? Pepper? Spice?"

"No, no. Nothing. It is full of *amor,* Tia, that is enough."

She swatted him on the arm. "You make fun of an old woman, Alejo."

"I don't," he protested. "It's your love, the secret ingredient, that makes it so delicious."

She flapped a dismissive hand at him, but her bosom swelled and she stood taller. He grinned inwardly. Women. You complimented their beauty when they were young, and their cooking when they got old. It was a simple formula to keep them happy.

"You like this outfit, *mi corazon?*"

*And sometimes you compliment both.* "It's very pretty. Slimming, too. You look beautiful, Tia." He moved on to a more serious subject. "The palm tree in the front yard—I think it's much too close to the house, and I'm worried it will fall on your roof in the next storm. I want to get a quote for removing it."

She frowned. "God put the tree there. It's not for us to take it out. If He wants it to fall, then it will be so."

"Yes, but, Tia, I don't want it to fall on your head one night when you're asleep." Alejandro put a hand on her arm. "Isn't it God who gave us the power-saw and the backhoe, too? Why would He have done that, if He didn't mean for us to use them? You've said so yourself—God helps those who help themselves."

"Hmph."

"And God brought me here to look after you. You wouldn't want to stand in the way of my doing that, would you?"

She eyed him suspiciously, hands on her hips.

He blinked, all innocence, his own hands spread and palm up in supplication.

"*Bueno*. Take out the tree."

"Thank you, Tia. We can go to the nursery when I have a free day and find something nice to replace it."

They chatted some more as she loaded up all the food in disposable aluminum containers. She gave him rapid-fire instructions for how to heat it again, and asked him about a couple of investments. Then she said, "You are still serving liquor at the salon?"

"Not liquor. Just wine and beer."

She shook her head and clucked. "I never hear of such a thing."

"That's because it's new. A fresh marketing angle. We stay open late and serve drinks. It's been very popular so far, Tia. Come on, wipe the frown off your face."

"A salon should be a salon, and not a bar!"

"People like it. It's getting busier and busier."

"Soon you will have a massage parlor in back."

"Well, Peggy does give massages, but—"

"You know what I mean, Alejo. You serve drinks, people *tocar por aqui, tocar por alla*, soon you have goings-on in the closet, the powder room, God only knows where."

He laughed. "I can promise you, *mi corazon*, there are no goings-on in closets. Absolutely not." He kissed her cheek. "Please don't worry, Tia. We have everything under control."

Alejandro thanked her for the food, stowed it in his

Porsche and got on his way, trying not to think about having a naked Kate under his control in a closet or a powder room. He couldn't wait to see her, even clothed and around her awful cousin.

# 7

KATE HAD ACTUALLY acquired a small kitchen table and four chairs from a furniture warehouse by the next day. They were streamlined, modern blond wood, some assembly required. The store had delivered them on the same day and they fit her needs perfectly, even if they weren't up to Wendell's standards. "Cheap and pedestrian," he pronounced them.

*Just like a Spinney.* She rolled her eyes.

Her mother had pronounced perms "cheap and pedestrian" back in their heyday, and when Kate had snuck out and gotten one anyway, she'd marched her by the ear back to the salon and made them straighten it again, then smooth it down with wax.

"Why did you invite this Eric Estrada person to dinner, again?" Wendell asked, disturbing her fond memories. "You don't have a thing for him, do you?"

"Stop calling him Eric Estrada!" said Kate. "And we're just classmates working on a project. Of course I don't have a thing for him." *Especially not if he's after my money.*

"Good. Because you can only imagine what the family would say."

Kate froze in the act of rinsing some lettuce and to-matoes—she figured the least she could do was make a salad. Alejandro was bringing everything else. "You know, Wendell, if I did choose to have a 'thing' for him, I really wouldn't give a hoot what the bloody family said."

"*Riiiiight.* You think they'd just ignore the fact that some low-life Spic—"

Kate gasped.

"—was moving in on a Spinney?" Wendell laughed. "Because I can assure you, they wouldn't."

Shaking with anger, Kate said evenly, "Wendell, call him a *Spic* again and you can get the hell out of my condo and never contact me again, you racist son of a bitch."

Her cousin leaned back in the kitchen chair he occupied, causing it to creak. He raised an eyebrow. "Touchy, touchy. Maybe you *doooo* have a thing for Al, or why would you care what I call him?"

"Because he's my *friend,*" Kate said, furious despite her own uncertainty about Alejandro's motives for getting to know her. "And because with your expensive education, you should be a little more enlightened."

This time, Wendell rolled *his* eyes and she wished passionately that they would just fall right out of his head and Gracious would snuffle them up as an after-noon snack. But the pig was sacked out on a couch pillow, snoozing.

Her cousin cast Gracious a glance of dislike. "Really, Kate. You probably have all kinds of vermin in here, now, because of that creature."

*Yup. There's one kind sitting right there, and it's*

*about five foot ten with pale blue eyes and an obnoxious personality.*

"You should seriously think about a goat and some chickens, just so the place will smell fab. Throw down some straw, too. Paint the door red. Sing 'Old MacDonald' when you get up in the morning…."

The phone rang before Kate gutted him with a paring knife or twisted a corkscrew into his skull. It was Kevin, the clerk from the reception desk downstairs, announcing that Alejandro had arrived.

She opened the door minutes later to find him on the other side with a large shopping bag, laden with containers of food. "Hi. Come on in. Can I take that from you?"

"Hi, Kate." He bent and kissed her cheek, Peruvian style. Her cousin looked on with a smirk.

"Wendell wants a kiss, too," she said provocatively.

Alejandro looked alarmed. "Sorry, but I just ran out. That was my last one." He grinned and shrugged, while behind her Wendell breathed a sigh of relief.

"I'm so glad to hear that," he drawled, "because Spinney men don't kiss men." He looked at Kate. "Well, unless they're her brother, Marcus."

"Let's leave Marcus out of this, shall we?" Kate said as pleasantly as possible.

"Whatever you say. Hey, something smells pretty good. I hear we're having a Third World feast."

Kate closed her eyes.

"No, we're having a Peruvian feast," Alejandro corrected him, a glint in his eye. "We'll start with *choritos,* or baked mussels with fresh salsa. Then we'll move on to the *cau-cau,* a type of…stew. And then there's the *escabeche de pescado,* a pan-fried fish with vegetables on top. I brought flan for dessert."

"Sounds delish," said Wendell. "Katy, shall I open a bottle of wine? Do you even have any decent wine?"

"There are two bottles of rioja in the pantry over there."

Wendell pulled them out and sniffed. "Table wine? 2003? Really, Kate."

She considered stoning him to death with canned goods she had in the hurricane-preparedness stash. But instead, she took a deep breath. "Sorry, Wendie—I'm fresh out of vintage Lafite Rothschild."

Alejandro's eyes danced. "What a shame."

Kate pulled three glasses from a cabinet and set them on the counter. "Do you want to just serve everything in here, Alejandro? The table's rather small."

*"Perfecto."* He began unloading aluminum containers from the shopping bag and setting them on the kitchen counter. "We'll need to warm the *escabeche* and the *cau-cau.*"

They put them into the oven and sat around the new table with their wine and some cheese. Kate tried not to look at Alejandro's sexy, exotic mouth or the triangle of lickable brown skin bared by the open top button of his shirt.

Her nerves were jangling, both because of Wendell's sniping and because of her unfortunate attraction to Alejandro. She might as well admit it—she thought the man was hot. In no way did he fit the stereotype of an accountant.

Kate tipped back a healthy amount of wine to (a)

calm down, (b) keep from killing her cousin and (c) stop herself from jumping onto Alejandro's lap and shouting, "Do me, do me, baby!"

She'd go to jail if she killed her cousin, and Wendell was *so* not worth spending one's life in jail for. As for option c, she'd be demonstrating serious lack of control, something quite alien to a Spinney.

She was spacing out. Kate checked into the conversation again only to find Wendell pontificating about Rembrandt—Rembrandt?—a subject that he knew nothing about but had undoubtedly chosen because he didn't think Alejandro knew anything about the artist, either.

Alejo exchanged an amused glance with her and smothered a yawn, before he got up ostensibly to check on the food. Kate drained the rest of her wine and poured everyone some more. Then she, too, abandoned her cousin and fled for the kitchen to get out her best china: paper plates. She did have real cutlery, cheap stuff she'd bought by the dozen at a restaurant supply store. And she tore them each a paper towel to use as a napkin.

Alejandro brought out the pan of *choritos* and set it in the middle of the table. "You just pick these up and eat them. They're a little tricky, but you can use your teeth to scrape the mussel off if necessary." He demonstrated while Wendell watched, aghast.

Kate handed him a paper towel and grabbed a *chorito,* inserting it inelegantly into her mouth and gobbling down the contents of the shell. It tasted fresh and delicious, the shellfish flavor mingling with lime juice, onion, tomato and cilantro. "Yum!"

Gracious emerged from Kate's bedroom with a yawn, stretching her short legs. She made a beeline for the table, saw Wendell sitting there, and drew back her lips in a funny porcine snarl.

"Get away from me," he said, and finally picked up a *chorito*. Kate laughed as it stretched his mouth wide, making him look like an outraged Mr. Potato Head. Not that she and Alejandro looked any better.

"This isn't half-bad," Wendell admitted. "Of course, I've had better in Rio."

"Really." Alejandro went to Gracious and scratched her head and neck while she wiggled her nose in appreciation of the food smells. She began to drool and edged toward the kitchen. But to enter the room, she had to squeeze past Wendell. She looked at him again and snarled.

"You're not being very gracious, Gracious," Kate said. She gave her a dried apricot.

Wendell glared at the pig. "You like dining with farm animals, Eric?" he asked. "Er, Alejandro?"

"It doesn't bother me. She's a very nice pig."

Wendell smirked. "Well, I guess you're used to eating in barnyards, since your family hails from a Third World village, right?"

Alejandro's face remained impassive.

"Don't be a boor, Wendell," Kate said as pleasantly as she could. "And Lima is not a village. It's a bustling, modern city, like Rio."

"I've traveled all over the world," Wendell announced in pompous tones. "I know Lima."

"Ah. Then you must have had *cau-cau,* one of our

popular dishes." Alejandro slopped a large ladleful onto a plate.

"Of course I have," lied Wendell. "It's delicious."

Alejandro added another ladleful. "Here you are." He passed the plate to Wendell, then turned to Kate. "Would you care for some?"

"You know, I think I'll wait for the *escabeche de pescado*—I won't have room for both." Alejandro nodded and helped himself to the *cau-cau*. They all sat down.

"I know you people are religious," Wendell sniped. "Should we say grace?"

Kate cringed, while Alejandro fought with a murderous expression and finally won. "No, that won't be necessary, but thank you for your, ah, cultural sensitivity."

"Please start," Kate urged them, raising her glass to her lips.

Wendell took a large bite of the *cau-cau*.

Alejandro did, too.

Wendell froze mid-chew.

Alejandro swallowed. "Wonderful," he said, beaming at her cousin. "One of my Tia Carlotta's best batches ever. But as a man of international cuisine, of course you recognize that."

Wendell's eyes had begun to bulge, but he nodded.

"Only sophisticated, well-traveled types such as yourself can appreciate the subtle flavors of a world-class *cau-cau*."

Wendell's face assumed a greenish hue, and beads of sweat formed at his temples and along his sparse hairline. With a mighty effort, he swallowed what was in his mouth. "Delish," he managed.

Alejandro nodded and kept eating heartily.

Kate watched with glee as Wendell's pride demanded that he eat what was on his plate, just to prove how cosmopolitan he was. He forked up another mouthful of *cau-cau* and inserted it into his pie-hole.

"You know," Alejo told him, "I'm impressed. A lot of gringos won't eat tripe, but you're clearly above that."

"Tripe," Wendell repeated weakly, after he barely managed to swallow his second bite.

"Parts are parts, my Tia always says. And *we people* don't like to waste anything. Sometimes her local butcher will throw in more than the stomach lining, just for her. You know, bits of other things that will add flavor—that's the secret of her *cau-cau*. Maybe the tail end of the small intestine, if you know what I mean. Or a bit of the bollocks.... Is something the matter?"

Wendell clutched his stomach and ran from the room as fast as his stubby legs would carry him.

"Was it something I said?" Alejandro asked, the barest twinkle in his eye.

WENDELL CLAIMED A twenty-four-hour stomach flu when he returned, still looking green. Kate offered, just a shade too earnestly, to make him chamomile tea, and he eyed the two of them suspiciously while Alejandro looked utterly bland and Kate did her best to be sweet. This only made Wendell's behavior worse.

He turned down the *escobeche de pescado* and the salad, glowering down the table at Kate, who ignored him. She got up and put together a plate of dried fruit and goodies for Gracious and set it down in the kitchen.

Again, the pig snarled as she approached Wendell and had to pass him to get to her food.

Already cranky, Wendell drew back a leg as if to kick her, only to stop as Alejandro got up and loomed over him. All traces of social nicety had vanished from Alejo's expression. In fact, he looked downright menacing.

"Touch that animal, *hombre,* and you will sincerely regret it."

Wendell sneered at him. "Don't you threaten me, you lowlife Spi—" He stopped as Kate whirled on him.

"It's not a threat, I assure you." Alejandro's voice was quiet. "It's a promise." He bent down and picked up Gracious, who looked as if she wanted to charge Wendell again.

"Put her in my bedroom," Kate told him quickly. "I'll take her plate in there." She did so then returned to Wendell again. "How dare you kick a defenseless animal?"

"I didn't actually kick it," Wendell retorted, getting up and throwing his crumpled napkin onto the table. "Not to mention that barnyard animals do not belong in a civilized home. But then, neither do savages from the back of beyond—"

Alejandro re-entered the room and stared him down, his gaze black.

"I never claimed to keep a civilized home," declared Kate. "Look, everyone, let's just calm down and have dessert, okay?" She reached for her wineglass.

"I don't think so," Wendell said. "I'm not eating any more of his Third World peasant food."

Alejandro took two long strides towards him, his fist drawn back.

Kate leaped towards him and planted a palm on his chest while her cousin scurried for the door, yanked it open and scrambled through. She slammed it behind him.

"Alejandro, I'm so sorry. He didn't mean that."

"Oh, yes, he did."

She made a helpless gesture. "Please—I know he's an ass. But he's gone for the time being. Let's just try to salvage the evening and enjoy dessert. What do you say?"

His face softened and he hesitated. Finally he nodded. While the coffee brewed, they sat down again with their wine, this time on the floor by the sliding glass door where they could take in the view of the ocean.

"So, do *you* have any horrifying relatives?" Kate asked him.

Alejandro shook his head. "I have an uncle in Peru who tells tall tales. And a shoplifting cousin. But other than that, they're really not that bad. Of course, Tia Carlotta can be a handful when she wants to be…."

"Oh. Lucky you." Kate swirled her wine. "So what do you do when you're not balancing people's books?"

A funny, discomfited look crossed his face. "I, uh, play *futbol*—soccer—for a local league. Most of us are Peruvians, but we also have a couple of Columbians and a Bolivian on the team. And I help out at Tia's house with repairs and projects. Other than that, business school takes all my time these days."

There was something he wasn't telling her. She said so. "Do you have a girlfriend?"

"No."

"A boyfriend?"

"*No!*"

"Then what is it?"

He spread his hands. "Nothing. What would I be hiding?"

"I don't know." She pursed her lips. "You don't look like a serial killer."

"Thank you."

"Or a pedophile."

"Kate! I'm not hiding anything."

"Are you after my money? Because it's all tied up in trusts anyway."

He gaped at her. "You are, without a doubt, the most insulting woman I've ever met."

"I'll take that as a compliment. So, are you? After my money?"

"*No.* Besides, I'd have to marry you to get it, and I don't think it would be worth the pain."

She grinned at that, studying his face. "I think I believe you."

"Yes?" He set down his wineglass. "Well, I think I want to leave now. I've taken enough *mierda* for one evening."

Kate put a hand on his arm. "I'm sorry. For everything, Wendell included. Please stay."

He relented. "Okay."

"Tell me more about yourself."

Alejandro picked up his glass again, tipped more wine into his mouth and thought about it. "I used to like to go out dancing. Do you salsa, Kate?"

She looked at him doubtfully. "I *eat* salsa. Does that count?"

He shook his head, laughing. "Do you samba?"

"Definitely not."

"Merengue?"

She shook her head. "And I don't hula, foxtrot, square-dance, or can-can, either. I may as well say that up front."

"Do you dance at all?"

Kate took a large sip of wine. "I have been known, when drunk, to do the funky chicken. I used to know the steps to the 'Time Warp' dance from the *Rocky Horror Picture Show.* And I was forced to learn the waltz before my—uh, I was forced to learn the waltz."

"Before your what? Wedding?" Alejandro grinned.

Ugh. It was worse. "No, I've never been married."

"So why did you have to learn the waltz?"

"For a formal party," she muttered, feeling her color rise. "Hey, we should get that coffee."

"The coffee can wait," he said. "And now *you're* hiding something."

"I don't know what you mean." She widened her eyes and sipped more wine.

He thought for a moment and then snapped his fingers. "You had to learn the waltz before your coming-out ball!"

She winced and felt her face flame. She tipped the rest of the wine down her throat.

Alejandro hooted. "Did you wear a lacy white dress? And a strand of pearls?"

She squirmed.

"You must have looked beautiful, my little debutante," he said. "But doesn't that up your shoe quota? It means you have a pair of white shoes, too."

"I burned them," she said darkly. "Because they hurt my feet so much. I couldn't walk the day after the party. So I tossed them into my bedroom fireplace."

"You had a fireplace in your bedroom?" Alejandro looked very intrigued by the thought.

"In Boston, yeah." She got up to pour them both some coffee, only to decide on more wine instead. She pulled the second bottle out of the pantry, and when she turned to find the corkscrew, she found herself looking straight at Alejandro's chest. His very sculpted chest.

Without thinking about what she was doing, she put out a hand to touch it, ran her fingers over the smooth muscles above his sternum and then down to the six-pack riding above his belt.

He sucked in his breath and let her explore, until her naughty fingers took a pass over a nipple—at which point he grabbed her wrists, pinned them behind her, and kissed her deeply and thoroughly.

Kate froze even as her mouth responded to his. She had no business doing this…Spinneys didn't grope men in kitchens…but then her body just took over. Life couldn't be all about business, could it? And besides, she was engaged in an anti-Spinney revolution. Surely kissing a hot man while wedged in her pantry got her one step closer to being Just Kate, the kind of woman who would dance on a table.

# 8

ALEJANDRO'S LIPS PARTED hers and his mouth took command. Kate could smell sweet, mild soap and tangy, breezy aftershave and a tinge of musk. She tasted the wine they'd both drunk, and found it intoxicating all over again.

As a modern woman, she could have objected to the fact that her wrists were imprisoned. But the fact was that it turned her on, just like his tongue making love to hers and the roughness of his stubble scraping her face and his growing erection pressing against her stomach.

Her body had an unprecedented response to Alejandro's, heat flashing through her like an electrical current. Her nipples pebbled, seeking attention, and something pulsed at the core of her.

He kept on kissing her, drinking her in, while she did that liquefication thing again. Her body loosened and warmed, molding to his.

Finally he let go of her wrists to explore the curve of her back, span her waist, and move downward to her hips. Still in possession of her mouth, he slid his big hands right down to her bottom and traced its contours.

Heat seeped through the fabric of her khakis and her white cotton panties. Alejandro squeezed, and brought her hard against his cock, rubbing against her.

Then those magic hands crept upward again. He broke the kiss, smiling as she sagged against him, her knees rubbery and her head feeling as if it could topple off her neck at any moment. He cupped her breasts—if you could call them breasts, they were more like fried eggs—and then stroked across her nipples with his thumbs, sending a streak of pure desire through her.

She inhaled sharply and pushed against his hands to encourage him. Then she wondered what the hell she was doing and pulled back.

"You started this, Kate," he murmured. "No fair if you get to touch mine and I can't return the favor." So saying, he flipped up the hem of her Polo shirt and found her breasts all over again, this time unhooking her bra with a smooth, one-handed maneuver. His palms mastered the little mounds immediately, and he rubbed lightly in a circular motion. It felt so good that she almost lost her footing.

"There isn't much there," she muttered, embarrassed.

"Shh. They're perfect. Bite size." And he shoved her shirt up to her neck and took one into his mouth.

Kate cried out, which surprised the hell out of her, and he bent her back so that he had a better angle. What if he dropped her? But as his tongue laved her nipple and he suckled her she somehow didn't care.

And fair was fair, so before he got to the other breast, she tugged his own shirt out of his waistband and finally touched his bare chest. He pushed her hands away and slipped his shirt completely off so that he stood half-naked before her, and Kate just stared.

He was beautiful. As fine as they came. She reached out to touch him, just to make sure he was real. Alejandro grinned at her, captured her hand and twined his fingers with hers. "I want to make love to you, Kate," he said, his dark eyes half-lidded and smoky and sexy as hell. "Right here. Right now."

Oh. Well. When he put it like that, how could she refuse? It would be…rude. Spinneys were never—wait, that was a lie. Spinneys could be *exceptionally* rude. Take Wendell, for example. But somehow she really wanted to mind her manners just now. So Kate blinked and then swallowed and then said, "Okay."

The word was barely out of her mouth when she thought of all the reasons she should *not* sleep with Alejandro. She had to see him in classes. They had the marketing project to work on. This was a very bad idea. But before she could retract her *okay,* he seized her, set her on the kitchen counter and stripped off her khakis.

He whipped off her shirt, tossed her cotton bra in the direction of the stove, positioned himself between her thighs and then began to systematically devour her.

He started with her eyelids, moved to her temples, down to her neck, back up to her ears. He took her left lobe between his teeth and bit it lightly as he abraded both of her nipples with his thumbs. Then he murmured, "Kate, *mi amor,* we are going to need a whole box of condoms. You have some?"

*Oh, no…why does protection always have to get in*

*the way of fabulous hot sex?* This was where things inevitably got awkward. She shook her head and groaned, searching for a solution. "Hey, maybe we could use plastic wrap?" She was only half kidding.

"Definitely not. It's a good thing that Boy Scouts and Peruvians always come prepared."

"What, you planned this?" He had closed his mouth over one of her nipples again, and while it felt exquisite, she needed to know. Kate grabbed his nose and pulled upward.

"Ow! Whad are you doig?"

"Did you plan to seduce me tonight?"

"A guy cad always hobe. Bud no, since your *primo horrible* was here, I did not."

"Does *primo* mean *cousin?*"

He nodded. "Now, will you led go of by dose?"

"Okay. I'll give you the benefit of the doubt." She released her grip.

Alejandro collapsed laughing on the counter, his forehead on the cool tiles. That put the top of his head right in her most private spot. She squirmed.

"I can honestly say, Kate, that nobody has ever grabbed my nose during sex."

"Oh." Her mouth quivered. "Well, was it a turn-on?"

That made him laugh even harder. "Not exactly."

"I'm sorry," she said in a small voice. "But see, I probably would have screwed this up anyway. I'm not very good at this stuff."

He raised his head at that. "What do you mean, you're not very good? At what stuff?"

"Well, um, sex."

He stared at her.

"You want to know the truth?" Kate asked, the wine obviously making her crazy. What had happened to her New England reserve?

"Yes."

"Okay. I've had sex with only three men."

He scowled. "I will kill them later. Go on."

"Well, the first time I didn't know what to do at all. So I didn't do anything, and he told me afterward that I was a lousy lay. Then the second guy—well, I was determined that nobody was going to say that about me again, so I was rather, um, active." She caught her lip between her teeth, squinted at him and asked, "Are you sure you want to hear this?"

He nodded.

"O—kaaay. Well, so I kind of bounced around a lot. And I, um, sprained his thing."

Alejandro blinked. "You *sprained* it?"

She winced. "Yeah. Please don't ask me how. I'll die if I have to go into details."

"So what happened with the third man, *mi corazon?*" His voice was unsteady with mirth.

"Hey! This isn't funny, you know."

"No. It's not, you're right. So go on."

She eyed him suspiciously to make sure he was properly serious about her trauma. Reassured, she continued.

"It was awful. The third guy…well, he stuck it in, but it lost all its, um, steam immediately and fell out. He blamed me. He said I looked more like a boy than a girl."

"That's ridiculous." Alejandro put his hands on either side of her face and kissed her soundly, even though her lower lip was quivering. "You're one hundred percent woman."

"Well, I'm not, exactly. My chest is practically concave, and I'm too skinny and—"

"Kate, your chest is not concave. What are these?" He held her breasts in his palms.

"Fried eggs? Twin lima beans?" She squeaked as he closed his mouth over one and gave it a thorough going-over. "What—"

He looked up at her and winked, then finally let go. "I'm just testing the seasoning," he explained. "And I think they need...*comino*."

"What?"

"Cumin. And cilantro, maybe."

"See, they're not spicy enough."

"Kate, *mi amor,* I was kidding. Now, listen to me. You are a beautiful, very desirable woman. In fact, I'm going to lick every inch of you, and probably twice. As for you not being *good* at making love, it just takes the right person. These men you have spoken about— imbeciles, every one of them."

"Drexel wasn't an imbecile. He was an M.I.T. graduate."

"Wait. You actually slept with a man named *Drexel?* Please tell me you're kidding. No, I can see by your face you are not. And you have a Wendell the fourth for a cousin. This should not surprise me."

"And Kippy had a Ph.D."

*"Dios mio. Kippy?"* He slapped his forehead.

"But you're right about Stone, I must say."

Alejandro burst out laughing. Then he pulled off her panties.

"Hey! Give those back."

"No. You won't be needing them for a while." Alejandro tossed them over his shoulder and they landed in Gracious's bowl of Mini Pig Chow. He slid his warm hands to the inside of her knees and worked the muscles there with his thumbs, easing the tension caused by her position but creating more tension inside her. She was open to him, he could see *everything* and she wasn't sure she was quite ready for that.

Instead of going straight to her radio dials, so to speak, to play with the knobs, he surprised her. His eyes grew dark, intense and carnal as he looked at her there, but he simply said, "Pretty," and moved his hands to her right calf, which he massaged all the way down to the ankle. Then he took her foot into those hands, and performed magic on it. Pure magic.

Kate had never in her life thought of her foot as a sexual organ until now. What he did to her toes, the ball, the instep, the arch...oh, heaven, the arch! And back down to the heel...it was indescribable.

"You like, *mi amor?*" he asked with a smile.

She was unable to speak; just nodded and moaned.

Alejandro seemed to appreciate her answer, since he bent and kissed her right *there,* and she almost came on the spot. But then he was massaging her other foot and she fell into the bliss of that. When he finally stopped and kissed her on the mouth again, she murmured, "Alejo, you could be a professional!"

He froze and then gave a short bark of laughter. "I don't think so. That is hardly a job for a man."

"What a shame," she said, "because I'd definitely give you a great reference."

"Heh, heh." But Alejandro didn't seem all that amused.

Kate reached to unfasten his pants. "So what's in here?"

"Ah. Behind that zipper, you will find a primo example of Peruvian sausage."

"Is it tasty?"

"Very." If possible, his eyes got even darker and more intense.

She wet her lips, reached inside his pants and took hold of it, impressed by its size and thickness. She squeezed.

"All right, that's enough of that," Alejo declared, removing her hand.

"What? Am I doing it wrong?"

"No, *mi amor.* I'm just not ready yet."

"I thought men were always ready for that...."

"Shh." He stroked her breasts again and then trailed his fingers down to her belly, ran them along her legs. The contrast of his warmth with the cold tiles under her bottom was highly sensual, and when he moved to the soft skin of her inner thighs she shivered. He brushed the curls at her apex and she began to tremble in anticipation.

It wasn't just the sensations he awoke within her, but the promise of his caresses to come. And the sight of his powerful, naked chest and taut stomach between her legs.

Alejandro bent his head, suckled her breasts and began to play his fingers against her private folds. Then he replaced his fingers with his mouth and she gasped in shocked pleasure. Drexel and Kippy had certainly never done *that*. Oh, my…

Kate clutched at Alejo's hair, his neck, his shoulders, while she tried to assimilate all the erotic sensations that his tongue and his clever mouth brought her. Finally she clutched at the counter on one side and a stove burner knob on the other side as he slid his hands under her cheeks and gripped her hard, holding her in place while she squirmed and thrashed under the sensual assault.

"Can't take anymore," she gasped, trying to twist away. In answer he swirled his tongue around her clitoris and she banged her head on something—the sugar canister?—while a wave of pure pleasure hit her between the legs, followed by another and another. She bucked uncontrollably against his mouth until she lay exhausted and he kissed her stomach. Slowly she became conscious that she held the burner knob in her left hand. She must have ripped it off.

To her embarrassment, Alejandro pried her fingers off it, chuckled and stuck it back onto the stove. "I'm glad it was not a frying pan, *mi corazon*. I'd have dents in my head or broken vertebrae."

Shame washed over her. "S-sorry. I don't know what happened there…."

"Don't ever apologize to a man who's brought you joy, hmm? To watch his woman climax is the highest compliment he can receive."

"Yeah?"

He nodded. Then he reached into his back pocket, pulled out his wallet, and dug out a condom. He unfastened his pants and pushed them, with his boxers, to the floor. He managed to get his shoes off at the same time he kicked out of the chinos. "Now, where were we?"

Kate just stared. And stared some more. He was magnificent, his smooth café au lait skin all one color from face to feet. No silly-looking tan lines on Alejandro. Nope. His thighs and calves were even more powerful than his chest, and it wasn't hard at all to picture him playing soccer. He was a man in peak condition with no fat on him at all that she could see.

"Kate?"

"Hmm?"

"Would you like to do the honors?" He held out the condom to her.

"I'll probably put it on backward." But she took it gingerly and caressed him with her other hand. Alejandro's eyes seemed to roll back into his head and he groaned. He took over operations and rolled the condom down the length of him. Then he kissed her, tugged her to the edge of the kitchen counter and slid inside.

She welcomed the slick fullness of him, wiggled to take even more of him in, and he picked her up and walked into the living room with her, dropping to the floor and rolling her under him.

Then he got down to work, creating a sensual shimmer as he stroked into her, melting things all over again. He took his time, his rhythm slow and languorous and deeply erotic. Perspiration beaded on his brow as he pulled out all the way, leaving only the tip of his cock nudging her. Then he slid in a ways, slid out again, his gaze never leaving her face. He used his fingers to bring her more pleasure, too, finally settling them on her belly while his thumb delicately stroked her clitoris.

Desire coiled deep within her and tension began to build again, demanding release. Alejandro groaned and seemed to lose some of his control, finally driving into her hard and fast, his back and buttock muscles bunched. He brought her legs up so that her ankles rested on his shoulders and pounded into her, slapping against her bottom.

Again, it was partly the picture he made that brought her to climax: all that unleashed male power and beauty between her legs, desperate for release into *her*.

Heat and friction splintered into a thousand tiny points of light and Kate exploded. Then he did, too.

Alejandro collapsed on top of her, breathing like a freight train, and she lay there in wonder that she had done that to him, had any sexual power over such an exotic, beautiful man.

# 9

ALEJANDRO KNEW HE HADN'T died and gone to heaven, but he'd come pretty damn close. Though he didn't want to move, wanted to remain inside Kate forever, it occurred to him that he might be crushing her. He was big enough that he might even be causing a Kate-shaped indentation in the hardwood floor.

He rolled so that she lay on top of him, and pushed her wild, tangled curls out of her face, tucking them behind her ears. Kate smiled and shifted, scraping his knee. He winced. "You need a rug, *mi amor,* if we are going to keep this up."

"Yeah," she agreed, reaching back to rub her tailbone. "I do. Of course, we could always use the bed like normal people."

"I'm not partial to what we use," Alejandro said, settling his hands on her small white bottom. "As long as I get to have you." He squeezed.

A thought came to him as they lay there on the floor, and he frowned. "Did you lock the door after the *primo horrible* departed?"

Her eyes widened. "I don't remember. I'll get up and check."

"In a moment," Alejandro said, tightening his hands on her delectable ass. He raised his head just enough to kiss her. Things had just started to heat up and get interesting again when the door did, in fact, open.

"Holy Mother of God!" Wendell said, and then shielded his eyes with his hand.

Alejandro thanked the saints above that their feet were to the door, so all the jerk could see was Kate's rear end, which was bad enough.

"Ever hear of knocking, Wendell?" Kate said through gritted teeth, without turning her head. "Give us a moment, would you?"

The *primo horrible* backed through the door again and shut it without comment.

"Permission to kill him?" Alejandro begged.

She shook her head, scrambling up.

"At least lock him out and come with me to the bedroom. Let me show you the horizontal samba and the Twist 'n' Shout."

Kate ignored him and raced around the condo instead, fishing her panties out of the Mini Pig Chow and grabbing the rest of her clothes and his. Her face burned bright red, the color of a nice marinara sauce.

"What's the big deal?" Alejandro said.

"Put your clothes on!" she hissed. "Big deal? The big deal is that I'm utterly humiliated, and Wendell has a big mouth! He'll probably announce this at the next family gathering, like Thanksgiving or a board meeting."

"Even he cannot be such an asshole!"

"Oh, yes, he can."

"I heard that!" shouted Wendell through the door.

"Bugger off, Wendie!" Kate yelled back, now fully clothed.

Alejandro shook his head and climbed into his boxers and chinos.

"If you want my discretion, Katy," Wendell called, "we may be able to come to an arrangement if you vote a few shares my way."

Alejandro turned a powerful glare on the door and cracked his knuckles. "Let me have him, *please*," he said to Kate. "Just for five minutes."

"Touch one hair on my head and I will sue you a hundred times over for assault and battery," Wendell declared bravely, through two inches of wood.

Alejo spat a long string of unsavory and uncomplimentary Spanish words. He took a menacing step toward the door.

"Don't even think about it," Kate told him.

Growing ever more confident, Wendell yodeled, "Yoo hoo! Everybody got their drawers on, now? Nice buns, Katy. Did you have a good time? Did you bring the barnyard animal in on the action? Does your cheap hunk come with Energizer batteries?"

Cheap hunk? *Batteries?* Alejandro leaped for the door, wrenched it open and made a grab for Wendell, who tore down the hallway as fast as his stubby legs would take him.

Kate followed, shouting. "No! Alejo, no!"

Ignoring her—after all, there was only so much a man could take—Alejandro caught the little turd within seconds and threw him against the wall, drawing back his fist.

Wendell squeaked, but his eyes were malevolent and more than a little excited.

"Don't do it! Kate shrieked. "You can't afford the lawsuit. He's baiting you on purpose, don't you see?"

Breathing hard, dying to rearrange the little *chivo's* face, Alejo made himself count to five. Then ten.

Finally he said, "Okay. But he's leaving, and he's leaving *now*." He spun the *primo horrible* and grabbed him by the belt and the collar. He lifted him clean off the ground and marched with him to the elevator, where he let go of his collar long enough to punch the button. Kate just stood there with her hand over her mouth.

Wendell started to protest vocally as he was manhandled into the car, until Alejandro roared, *"Silencio!"* Neither of them enjoyed the ride down, but Alejo did enjoy stalking with his prisoner past the concierge desk and towards the main entrance.

"S-sir?" ventured a man in uniform behind the desk.

"You forgot to put this out with the garbage." And so saying, Alejo pushed out of the glass doors and deposited Wendell the fourth on a convenient bellman's cart. Then he brushed his hands together and walked back inside.

Kate appeared at the main elevators with wild hair and bare feet, just in time to see Wendell, spread-eagle and belly-down on the cart, roll down an incline.

"Maybe this will teach you to not to abuse your cousin's hospitality and to keep your mouth shut," Alejandro growled. *"Vete al Diablo,* eh?"

KATE ORDINARILY DIDN'T hold with excessive displays of macho, alpha-male behavior: chest-pounding and all that. But she had to admit to a tiny thrill—okay, it wasn't so tiny—that Alejandro had taken charge of the situation, namely exterminating her condo of Wendell.

Like some kind of knight, he had defended her honor—and Gracious's honor, too. He had also exercised his own aggression, but she figured that knights were pretty much entitled to that, as long as they claimed the higher motives.

Beating the crap out of the other guy had to feel good, and if you could spin it so that you did it in the name of honor, justice or religion then so much the better.

As a Harvard-educated Spinney, she strongly believed in women standing on their own two feet, but gazing at Alejandro's still bare chest, now glistening with perspiration and pumped up from exertion, she found that she also strongly believed in…disgusting displays of excess testosterone. Really, what could be yummier?

She discovered as well that she believed in hot, sweaty, screaming sex. So she took Alejo by the hand and tugged him back into the elevator, up the several floors to her condo and into her bedroom. Then she hurtled at him, knocked him onto her mattress, pulled off his pants again and did her very best to sprain his thing.

Gracious had taken one sniff at the air, figured out what was going on, and trotted out of the room. Obviously she was a pig with delicate sensibilities.

Luckily, Alejandro's thing was made of sturdier stuff than Kippy's thing. In fact, Alejo managed to wipe her mind clean of Drippy Kippy's image, flat on his back howling and gripping his man-root. The unfortunate scenario had haunted her for years.

They ignored the constantly ringing phone, figuring that it was Wendell trying to express his outrage, and finally ate dessert at about 3:00 a.m.

Gracious danced around drooling in hopes of table scraps, but was sorely disappointed. Kate was bending down to put a couple of dried apricots and some grapes into her bowl when Alejandro came up behind her and goosed her with Mr. Happy. "Wait," she said, grabbing it absently. "We never took Gracious out this evening. But she doesn't seem to need to go. Weird."

She didn't seem to have gone anywhere in the apartment, either, but Alejandro distracted Kate from thinking about it too much. His cock twitched in her hand, obviously ready to rock 'n' roll again.

"I guess I'm not as bad at this sex thing as I thought, huh?" she asked a little shyly. "Or maybe he's just not picky."

"He's very picky," he promised. "I'm fighting off women all day, in my line of work." Alejo's expression changed suddenly from teasing to serious, and he shut his mouth with a snap.

"Really. As an accountant?" Kate eyed him suspiciously.

"Well, er. You know. When I'm at the spa, doing the, uh, books. Some of the customers are a little forward."

Jealousy did a nasty little jig in her stomach. And he was hiding something again. The awkward pause, the hasty, lame explanation—they told the story. But what was he covering up?

She told herself she didn't need to know everything about him. After all, this was just a fling. So she said casually, "Fighting off women, huh? Well, you *are* pretty hot. They probably can't help themselves, right?" She poked him in the chest with an index finger.

He ignored the question and poked her with something else. "Got a garage for my hot-running engine, *mi amor?*" He grinned.

*Mi amor.* It sounded so sexy coming out of his mouth. "I don't know. Did you make an appointment to have it inspected?"

"Yes, as a matter of fact I did."

"Do you think it might just need a little oil?"

"I think that's exactly what it needs." He grabbed her and tossed her over his shoulder, making for the sliding glass doors that led out onto the balcony. "Put me down!" she shrieked. "We can't do this *outside*. Are you crazy?"

"What do you think balconies are for in south Florida, eh? Not just smoking cigars." He opened the door and tried to step out, but she hung on to the frame. "Don't be difficult, Kate."

"I excel at being difficult. And I am not having sex with you on this balcony!"

"Why not? It's dark. It's cool. There's a very nice view."

"It's not that dark anymore! It's five-thirty and the sun will be coming up soon."

"What could be more beautiful than making love at sunrise on a balcony overlooking Biscayne Bay? Now, shh." He peeled her hands off the doorframe, slid the door closed and lay down with her on top of him.

The night breeze caressed her naked skin and she could hear the waves below. Night creatures made their odd, mysterious music, ensconced in trees and bushes, and she forgot some of her discomfort just listening to them. Alejandro stroked the back of her neck, sending shivers down her spine, and then moved his strong fingers into her hair, massaging her scalp.

She relaxed, letting tension slip away with his touch. "*Ohhhhh.* God, Alejo, where did you learn how to do that?"

He didn't answer, just kept stroking and kneading all over her head until he was back at her neck again. From there he moved down to her shoulders and slowly rubbed and circled there, too, eventually going all the way down her spine to her bottom. Then he urged her forward and took her breast into his mouth, sucking and gently biting and laving her nipple until she whimpered and he took the other one, moving his hands down possessively to her ass.

Alejandro was a man who took his time. He believed in thoroughness, in the power of sensual, not just erotic, touching. As he kissed and licked and teased, he explored every inch of her thighs, every inch of her derriere, brushing gently down the private channel with his fingertips and setting her once again on fire.

He parted her, slipping two fingers inside, discovering that she was more than ready for him. And then he tilted her hips, positioned her so that she could sink down onto him. It felt so good, so right, so complete for him to fill her that way.

He caught her hands as he began to pump his hips upward. "Show me where to touch you," he whispered. "Teach me how to drive you wild."

Embarrassed, she didn't know what to do. She'd only gotten naked in front of him for the first time tonight. Yes, they'd achieved a certain level of intimacy, but there were certain things that were just private.

"Touch yourself," he urged her. "It's very sexy."

"You're kidding, right? I mean, if I touch myself, doesn't that imply that you're not doing your job?"

His teeth flashed white in the moonlight. "Not at all, *mi amor*. You're turning me on when you touch yourself. And you're helping, which is always good. And finally, there's a certain deliciousness about a woman who knows how to please herself."

Kate felt a little dubious about her, uh, deliciousness. She almost snorted, trying to imagine a man of Anglo-Saxon descent instructing her to explore her *deliciousness*. But when Alejandro said the words, they didn't sound silly at all.

She freed her hands from his and trailed them up to her breasts, looking carefully for his reaction. His mouth opened just a little, and his breath came a fraction faster. She rolled her nipples between her fingers and leaned back, taking his cock farther inside and plunging down on him at a different angle. He groaned.

She squeezed her breasts hard, and then, keeping one hand playing with them, she dropped her other one down to her mons and trailed her fingers against herself, sliding up and down, up and down. She spread her fingers so that they rubbed on either side of his cock as he pumped in and out of her, and he muttered something unintelligible, but grateful.

His eyes had closed and his chin jutted up at her,

where she saw a small white scar for the first time. Kate bent forward and kissed it. His eyes flew open. Still keeping one hand on herself, she reached in back of her with the other and lightly massaged his balls.

His reaction was instantaneous: he drove upwards in two consecutive mighty thrusts and spilled himself into her, calling her name.

Kate climaxed immediately after he did, the violence of her reaction shaking her like a rag doll. She fell forward onto his chest and listened to his heart galloping inside. Her own heart was doing much the same thing, but it wasn't only from the sex.

She looked around in wonder that she'd actually done this outside on the balcony for any passerby to hear or see. Spinneys definitely didn't do it outside. But…Just Kate apparently did. She wasn't sure if she was exactly *proud* of her actions, but she did feel inordinately free. A woman who could make love on a balcony could surely dance on a table.

# *10*

IT WAS UNFORTUNATE that Wendell didn't ride the bell-man's cart all the way back to Boston. Instead, he showed up at Kate's condo again the next day.

For reasons unknown to her, she let him up, put Gracious in her bedroom and opened the door purely out of misplaced guilt. He *was* family, and she'd let Alejandro throw him out of her building.

She wondered where her cousin had slept last night and hoped he'd had to pay a steep hotel bill. "Wendell, if you don't behave yourself, you can't stay here." She blocked the doorway.

Despite her words, he tried to barge past her. "I'm a relative. You can't kick me out."

She stood her ground. "You were *despicable* last night."

"Funny, I thought your stud was de Spic. And *I'm* not the one who resorted to violence. Very in character for his sort—"

Kate gasped in outrage.

"—those people are all the same."

"Wendell! Alejandro is normally harmless, but you would incite a *nun* to murder."

"Let me in, Katy, or I'll press charges against your Latin Lover. How would you like that?"

She grabbed his arm. "You wouldn't dare."

He smirked and sauntered past her, making himself at home in a kitchen chair.

Kate put a hand to her suddenly throbbing temples, knowing she'd never get him to leave before he was good and ready, the blackmailing jerk. But she couldn't let him cause trouble for Alejandro.

"Wendell, why are you really in Miami? I came down here to get *away* from the family. Are you just here to make my life miserable?"

"I'm here," he said smugly, "to do due diligence on a company Spinney Industries is thinking of acquiring."

She sank into a chair opposite him. "Why didn't they just ask *me* to do it, for God's sake? I'm already here."

"You made it very clear that you wanted nothing to do with the company's day-to-day operations for now. You're on the shit list, Katy. I'm their golden boy."

"Well, then, Golden Boy, you can move out of my spare bedroom and take advantage of your golden expense account, because if you haven't figured it out yet, you have gotten on my last nerve!"

Wendell yawned, got up and peered into her refrigerator. "No, I'll be staying for another couple of days—if you don't want your stud in jail. I'd be lonely in a hotel, Katy. Here, I have the pleasure of your company." He rubbed his plump stomach and pulled open her meat-and-cheese drawer. "I'm in the mood for a muffaletta. Want to make me a muffaletta?"

Kate didn't bother to answer him. She just grabbed her beat-up purse, shoved her feet into her loafers and walked out, slamming the door behind her. Wendell might be blackmailing her so he could stay in her condo, but that didn't mean she had to stay there with him.

She might as well get a start on the marketing project.

ALEJANDRO THANKED GOD that today was not tomorrow, when the Fabulous Four, a group of crazy forty-something women, would come in to have their weekly happy hour in the salon.

They scheduled their weekly manicures, pedicures, eyebrow waxes and haircuts on Thursday evenings, and enjoyed them with a considerable amount of After Hours wine. The Fab Four were wild, unpredictable and hard to handle.

The last time they'd been in, they'd gotten too drunk to drive and he'd been hornswoggled into taking them partying on South Beach, instead of to their homes.

So far, today was relatively peaceful. He was giving his sixth pedicure, to a sweet client who was not, thank God, wearing a miniskirt. Alejandro was just finishing up her foot and calf massage when Shirlie knocked and stuck her head in.

"*Al-aaaay-ho,*" she sing-songed, snapping her gum. "There's some girl up front named Kate—"

"*What?*"

"—asking a bunch of questions about the business. Peggy said you'd want to know."

Alejandro leaped up from the pedicure seat as if it were burning his butt. *"Carajo!"*

*"Perdon?"* said his sweet client, Dana Gomez.

*"Mierda!"* He stared down at her and clutched at his hair, getting lotion into it so that it stood on end. "Oh, sorry. Ah…will you excuse me for one moment?"

She nodded.

Shirlie snapped her gum again, eyeing him avidly. "Problem?"

"Yes! No! Yes!" What the hell was he going to do? Kate couldn't see him like this. But he couldn't walk out on his appointment…

"Shut the door," Alejandro said to Shirlie.

But she was talking into her earpiece. "After Hours, may I help you? Yes, she's here. Just a moment."

*"Carajo! Shut the—"* He started to get up.

"Is that Alejandro I hear?" Kate's voice traveled to his ears from the hallway, and then her crazy mop of hair came around the corner, followed by the rest of her. "Hi, Alejo! I didn't expect to see you—"

He was still bent over Dana's foot, caught red-handed unless he could think of some way to avoid disaster. Beauty Boy! Beauty Boy! The old taunts echoed in his ears, and he imagined Kate's contemptuous expression if she found out he was licensed to file.

He thought wildly, then said in a loud voice, "Just keep this foot elevated, Señorita Gomez. I've had some medical training, so I know what I'm doing."

"What?" Dana stared at him as if he had nine heads.

"I don't feel any broken bones, but it's probably best to get it X-rayed." He aimed a benevolent smile at her and patted her knee before looking up. "Oh, hello, Kate. What are you doing here?"

"I just came by to get started on the marketing project. I figured I'd ask Peg and Marly some questions."

Conveniently, his two partners popped into the hallway behind Kate and he sent them a death stare. They threw up their hands silently, denying any wrongdoing. "We had no idea she was going to stop by. Isn't it a nice surprise?"

"Yes, very nice," he said breezily. "That's, uh, great, Kate. Very proactive of you. I do wish I could stay and help. But unfortunately, we've had a small accident here—Miss Gomez has twisted her ankle. I'm going to have to run her to the minor emergency center."

"You are?" Dana asked.

Alejandro turned, met her bewildered gaze and sent her a look of desperate entreaty. "Yes, I'm afraid it's necessary. Just to make sure that there isn't some kind of hidden injury."

Dana played along, to his everlasting gratitude. "Well, if you think so…"

Shirlie snapped her gum and looked at her watch. "But Alejo, you have another—"

"Shirlie, I think there's a customer up front."

"Oh, okay, but—"

"Looking very impatient."

"Well, I was just going to tell you that—"

"And isn't that the phone ringing again?"

"Uh-huh, but—"

Marly dragged her away, thank God.

"You never told me you'd had medical training," Kate said, admiration in her tone, while a muffled snort came from Peggy's direction.

Alejandro ran a hand along the back of his neck. "Um, yeah. I was pre-med for a while in college."

"But you switched?"

He nodded. "To finance."

"With a minor in undertaking," Peggy added helpfully. "He really enjoyed dissecting the corpses in his medical classes."

"Ew," said Kate and Dana at the same time. Then Kate frowned. "I didn't know the University of Miami offered a minor in undertaking."

"That was a joke," Alejandro said quickly, his eyes narrowed on Peggy, conveying promises of torture later. "Peg has a strange sense of humor. It gets her in trouble a lot."

His partner shrugged and returned his glare blandly.

"Well, gosh, here we are standing around chatting while poor Dana is in such pain," Alejandro said. "We really should go."

His client produced a creditable moan and laid a limp hand on his arm. Excellent. He'd have to give her a free mani and pedi for her good sportsmanship.

"Do you need some help?" Kate asked, not looking exactly thrilled as he slipped one hand under Dana's knees and the other around her waist to hoist her up. Was she jealous? The thought pleased him.

Dana moaned again, a little too dramatically, and clutched at his chest.

"No, no, that's okay. But thanks." And feeling like

the king of all idiots, Alejandro strode out of After Hours with his armful of woman.

"Look at him. He's such a white knight," Peggy called after them. "Isn't that just the sweetest thing?"

He gritted his teeth. He'd deal with Peg later, when he had more time to kill her in slow, imaginative ways. For now, he had to concentrate on spinning yet another lie—this one to convince Dana that he wasn't certifiably insane.

He deposited her into the passenger seat of the Porsche, having no idea where to take her, what to do with her, or how to explain to his next appointments why he was standing them up.

Alejandro sighed. At least his day couldn't get any worse.

IT WAS WITH a sense of total injustice and panic that he heard Shirlie's words a few hours later.

"*Al-aaaaay-ho!* There's a guy up here for you. Name's Luis."

The goalie from his soccer team. *Mierda!* Alejandro scrambled to his feet from the pedicure stool. *What have I done to piss off God today? I can't even buy a break!*

"He said he saw your car out front as he was headed over to Benito's and he wants to see you."

"Tell him—" Alejandro thought frantically. "Tell him I'm on the computer. And I'll be right there." He turned to his client. "*Mi corazon,* will you excuse me, just for a moment? My apologies."

She nodded, and he sidled carefully out of the room

and darted into the salon's men's room, where he brushed nail particles off his shirt and scrubbed his hands to make sure there were no traces of nail polish anywhere. Then he took a deep breath and went to greet his visitor, a stocky man of about six feet who seemed entranced by Shirlie's bosom. A lot of men found Shirlie's terrain luscious, so Alejandro couldn't blame him. He saw no reason to ruin his fantasies by telling him that she wore a water bra that sloshed audibly when she ran for the phone from across the salon.

"Luis!" he said in deep, hearty tones. "*Como estas,* my friend?" All Luis knew was that Alejandro had a part interest in a spa and supervised the accounting and business decisions. He intended to keep it that way.

"*Bien, y tu?* What are you doing, working at eight o'clock at night? Come have a *coktelito* with me over at Benito's."

"Eh, Luis, I have far too much to do."

"*Sí,* and it will all still be here tomorrow. Come on, have a *pisco* sour or two with your teammate."

Alejandro hesitated, but he needed to get Luis out of the spa right away, before his next client came and blew his cover. "Okay. You go on over there, and I'll shut down the computer and join you in a moment."

Behind the counter, Shirlie opened her mouth to remind him of his next appointment and Alejandro sent her a death stare. Shirlie didn't always play with a full deck, but even she caught his meaning this time: shut up.

"Will you order for me, Luis? Be right there." He waved him out. As soon as the door shut behind him,

Alejandro turned to the receptionist. "Shirlie, you will have to cancel my next appointment."

"You've already missed two today and it's Heather Carlton. She's on her way to some party and she'll be really pissed off!"

"I can't help that. It will look too weird to Luis if I don't join him. And he cannot know, do you understand, Shirlie?"

"What about—"

"Can Peggy finish up with my current appointment? It's just the polish. It'll take her five minutes."

Shirlie sighed. "Okay. Yeah, she can probably do that. She won't be happy, though. She's got her own clients."

"She deserves it," he growled, thinking of retribution. "Say I was called away for an emergency. I'll see you in a bit." And he was out the door.

# *11*

BENITO'S WAS AN Italian restaurant only two businesses down in the strip mall, and Alejandro, Peggy and Marly ordered food from there all the time.

The place was decorated with red-and-white-checked tablecloths, fake grapevines with clusters of rubber grapes and empty chianti bottles on the tables that served as candlesticks. Benito used to have full bottles hanging at intervals along the vines overhead, but since the Case of the Concussed Customer he'd taken those down.

Benito, a small round Italian man with thinning black hair, greeted him as soon as he walked in the door. "Alejo! You are working hard, eh? Keeping all those ladies happy?"

He nodded and smiled, pumping Benito's hand. "We try. How are you, Benny? I'm just joining my friend Luis at the bar this evening."

"God has smiled upon my cooking again. Don't miss the fresh seafood cannelloni, my friend. In a white wine cream sauce that is a miracle of culinary perfection." He kissed his fingers. "Even my wife stopped nagging when she tasted it. You believe that? For an hour straight! I said it's a miracle, no?"

Alejandro laughed and slapped him on the back. Then he moved into the bar and settled down opposite Luis in a banquette. "So, how's the real estate business?"

"Excellent. I cannot complain." Luis picked up his glass and held it up. Alejandro followed suit and they did the traditional Peruvian toast. "*Arriba!* (Up!) *Abajo!* (Down!) *Al Centro!* (To the center!) *Adentro!* (Inside!)"

"And how is the spa business?" Luis asked. "Have you had your weekly mud bath and manicure?" He winked and laughed uproariously. Alejo's teammates loved to tease him about the feminine nature of his investment, but of course they didn't know the extent of his involvement.

Alejandro sighed inwardly, wishing that he could be done with all the pretense and sneaking around. But that was impossible. He waved a dismissive hand at Luis and shot him a friendly insult. "*Huevon.*"

"I am not the *huevon,* my friend. It's you who are the lone testicle!"

"*Sí,* and I'll be laughing all the way to the bank when we franchise After Hours all over the nation."

"Me, I am already laughing. South Florida real estate is a very nice business to be in." Luis grinned and admired his new gold Rolex.

Alejandro didn't begrudge him his success. He toasted him with his *pisco* sour.

"So, I want to get my girlfriend a gift, Alejo. You have a good all-day package at your spa?"

Mid-swallow, Alejandro choked at the question. All he needed was Luis's girlfriend booking anything with Señor Manos. It didn't bear thinking about.

But he nodded. "*Sí,* of course we do." He dug a card out of his wallet and handed it to his buddy. "You call and ask for Shirlie. She'll set it all up for you. I'll tell her to give you a good deal." *And I'll arrange to be gone that day.*

"*Gracias.* So, any *carne fresca* at the salon? Since you ended things with the woman in the twelve-step program for shoe addiction?"

Alejo grinned and stared down at his glass. He swirled the last inch of *coktelito* in it. "Yes. Her name is Kate. She is very intriguing. And she owns fewer shoes than any other woman I've ever met."

"To Kate." Luis held up his glass, and they toasted. "*Arriba! Abajo! Al centro! Adentro!*" Both of them drank and then ordered another round.

"So tell me about this Kate. She has *tetas grandes?*"

Alejandro shook his head.

"She is a former Miss Universe?"

"No. She is beautiful, but in a different way. She's... unique. Very refreshing."

"Where did you meet her?"

"Business school. And she's not at all the sort of woman I usually date. She needs a manicure desperately, she has crazy hair and she wears shoes that are falling apart."

"Okay," said Luis. He cocked his head and looked at him for a moment. "This doesn't bother you?"

"No. But she's too rich."

Luis went into peals of laughter. "Alejo, there is no such thing as too rich."

"No, you don't understand—her family is a dynasty that owns entire towns."

"Excellent. When's the wedding? You'll be set for life." Luis chuckled. "Get a nice, cushy job with Papa's company and learn to play golf. Join one of the, how do they say? Ritzy country clubs."

Alejandro didn't laugh with him. He thought instead about spending the rest of his life with people such as Wendell the fourth. He shuddered. There wasn't enough money in the world worth that.

"I see you're thinking very hard about it, my friend." Luis took a long swallow of his second whiskey, leaned back in the booth and fished a cigar out of his pocket.

"Benito will have a coronary if you light that in here. You have to go outside. And, no, I'm not thinking about marrying Kate for her money. You know the old saying—people who marry for money end up earning it."

Luis gnawed on the end of the cigar, looking very much like a camel with his long, blunt-tipped nose. "*Muy profundo,* Alejo. Well, don't get so involved with this girl that you don't make it to practice. We need you scoring goals in the Weston game."

Alejandro just shot him a look, as a female voice behind him said, "Oh, yeah, this looks like quite the emergency."

*Heather Carlton had come into Benito's for take-out.* He stared at her stupidly for a moment. Then he said, "Heather! It's not what it looks like. My friend Luis, here, just had tragic news."

Luis's eyebrows shot up and he took the cigar out of his mouth, but Alejo kicked him in the shin before he could say anything. "His father died suddenly of a heart attack. He is heartbroken. I had to comfort him."

Luis obliged him by doing his best to make his face look properly lugubrious. He even pretended to wipe a tear from his eye. Luis could lie to women with the best of them. And he didn't even work in the beauty industry.

Heather put her hand to her mouth and gasped. "Oh, you poor thing! I'm so, so sorry." She put her hand on his shoulder and kissed his cheek.

Luis stared straight into her cleavage as she did so, his interest sparking. Shirlie went by the wayside. Alejandro didn't want him and Heather to get any better acquainted, though. So he said, "Luis doesn't speak any English, but he knows what you mean. He thanks you for your sympathy."

Luis opened his mouth to deny his ignorance of English and perhaps ask for her phone number, but Alejandro kicked him again, hard.

"Aaaggh."

"That's Bolivian for *beautiful,*" Alejo told the client.

She put a hand to her heart. "Oh, how sweet. Too bad he doesn't speak any English. He's so cute…"

Luis sat there doing his best not to look gratified at her words since he wasn't supposed to be able to understand them. Luis was a good friend, taking one for his wingman.

Thanks be to God, Benito called Heather's order number and she told Alejandro to tell Luis how nice it had been to meet him, even under the terrible circumstances. Then she turned and walked away to the takeout window.

Luis watched her ass covetously, like a cat watches a goldfish. "A hell of a time for me not to speak any English, Alejo! What was that about?"

"She's a psychopath," Alejandro whispered. "You

can't believe anything that woman says. And trust me, you do not want to date her. Besides, what about your girlfriend?"

"Who?" Luis sucked on his cigar. "Oh. Her. Right."

By the time Luis was ready to leave, they'd each had three *pisco* sours and Alejandro was in danger of missing a fifth appointment. As it was, he was going to need to drink a quart of mouthwash. But hell, most of his clients would be tipsy, too, so he hoped no one would notice.

Unfortunately, Peggy did notice. It took her about two seconds to assess his general sobriety, and she hauled him into the kitchenette to talk. "Alejo!"

*"Sí?"* He tried to focus on her red hair, which she'd piled on top of her head. It was better than meeting her eyes. "Don't you look pretty tonight."

"Save the blandishing for the customers, honey. Did you just blow off an appointment to go drink with your friend?"

*"Shoccer* team," he said solemnly. "Had to get him out of here. Can't know truth."

"Alejandro. If I had done that, you'd never let me hear the end of it. That's terrible business practice. Heather Carlton screamed blue murder at Shirlie and accused us of trying to ruin her evening since she had two broken nails and couldn't go out like that. Shirlie said she even threatened to sue."

*"Sue?* For what?"

"Breach of contract or something crazy. I finally had to do her manicure myself. Oh, and she thinks you're avoiding her."

Alejandro sighed and scrubbed a hand over his face.

"You're going to have to call her and apologize."

"I, er, bumped into her at Benito's. Everything's fine."

"Look, Alejandro. We all think you're being ridiculous about keeping your work here a secret. Why don't you just tell people?"

"Are you *insane?*"

"No. Are you so insecure with your manhood that you can't handle people knowing the truth? That yes, you're a partner but you're also doing your best to make the place a success—so you take appointments. Where's the shame in that?"

"I am not the least bit insecure in my manhood," Alejandro declared.

"Yeah? Then why do you care what anyone says?"

"You don't understand Latin—and especially Peruvian—culture. It's simply not acceptable for a straight man to be a manicurist."

"That's so silly!"

"It's not. They will think I'm gay, like Nicky. The soccer team—they wouldn't allow me in the locker room or the showers."

"But why not, if you explained?"

"I am telling you, there *is* no explaining!" Alejandro searched for a way to make her understand. "It would be like…like…a church finding out that its head Sunday-school teacher was also a dominatrix and wore black rubber panties with a slit crotch."

"Oh, *puh-lease,* Alejandro. It couldn't possibly be that bad."

"It is. I don't know how to make you believe me. But it is."

"Whatever." Peggy put her hands on her hips. "But you can't go canceling appointments every time someone who knows you comes into the spa. You wouldn't let me do it, and I'm not going to let you do it. Understand?"

He stared at her, trying to remember why he was angry with her to begin with. Because he was, and it didn't have anything to do with tonight, but the *pisco* had fogged his brain. "Fine."

Then he remembered, and glared at her. "But by the way, we need to have a little talk, Miss Underwood. I can't believe that you and Marly actually suggested to Kate that we use After Hours as the business for our marketing class project! Are you deliberately trying to embarrass me in front of her?"

"If you hadn't lied to her in the first place, you'd have nothing to be embarrassed about," Peggy said, with maddening logic.

"That is not the point!"

"Isn't it?"

"No. The point is that you two maliciously plotted to make me crazy, and I don't appreesh—appreeski—*mierda!* It wasn't very nice."

Peggy neatly sidestepped that issue. "If Kate truly cares about you, then the fact that you give manicures and pedicures shouldn't bother her."

"Well, what if it does?" he asked belligerently.

"Then you're better off without her and we've only done you a favor."

Alejo frowned. He didn't think he agreed. But he decided he needed more rum in order to make sense of it all. He looked at his watch. Only ten, damn it. He still had two appointments to go before they closed for the night. "Peggy, sweet Peggy?"

"No," she said, without turning around. She was, disturbingly, pouring water into the coffeemaker.

"Have I mentioned that you look *partickly* lovely this evening?"

"I am *not* doing your last two pedicures. You know I'd do them if you were sick, or if you had exams tomorrow. But you don't—you're just drunk. So have some coffee and sober the hell up."

What had happened to his woman-manipulating abilities? He'd better sharpen them before he saw Kate again. Gloomily, he wondered why he cared. After all, as her cousin had said, he was nothing but a *cheap hunk,* a fling to her, and he knew it. Sighing, Alejandro lurched forward and got a big mug.

# *12*

"So, what is your competition like?" Kate asked Marly and Peggy. After Hours had been way too chaotic the other day to take up their time, so they'd all agreed on an appointment when the spa was closed.

Kate looked around the now quiet, empty spa, noting the eclectic Italian glass lighting, the beautifully hand-painted floors and the walls done in different Miami pastels. The whole place was hip and creative, the music international and energetic, cutting edge.

She balanced a yellow pad on her knee and spun a ballpoint pen in her right hand as she waited for Marly and Peggy to answer. "And where's Alejandro?"

"I don't know," Peggy answered, looking at her watch. "But he wasn't feeling so hot yesterday."

"Our competition," said Marly, "is pretty fierce around here. A lot of rich and famous people have homes in Miami, so to meet their demands there are dozens of high-end salons. We don't try to compete with the ones that cater to people like Madonna or Celine Dion. Our target customer is well-off, but not necessarily a millionaire. She's looking to be pampered, but she's also intrigued by a hip, party atmosphere.

She's not into whale sounds and total relaxation—she wants stimulation and excitement."

"Got it," Kate said, busily taking notes. "Now, do your customers drive long distances to get to you, or are they mostly in Coral Gables and the surrounding areas?"

Peggy pursed her mouth. "I'd say our clientele is mostly local. We do have a few women who drive from suburbs like Weston or Coral Springs or Parkland, but they represent only about twenty percent of our client base."

"So your customers are mostly women?"

"Yes," Marly said. "We're starting to see more men coming for haircuts and massages. But roughly ninety percent are women."

"Very key point," Kate murmured. "Are they married?"

Peg thought about it. "About fifty-fifty."

"Age?"

"Average age is from twenty-two to mid-fifties."

"Kids?"

"Also about fifty-fifty. If our customer has children, though, she's usually got help. She's still very body-conscious and fashionable. Our Coral Gables mom is not your average soccer mom. She's very likely to wear her spike-heeled mules and her Vuitton bag—with snug jeans—to the athletic fields."

"So there's no letting yourself go after kids. Poor things," Kate said. "They still have to be sex symbols?"

Marly shrugged. "Well, it's hot down here. Which means no hiding fat under sweaters and coats and layers of wool. Skin is in, and cellulite's not popular."

"And there's a lot of South American influence," Peg added. "Those women are gorgeous and they take care of themselves. They're sexy, even after four kids."

Kate wrote it all down. She chewed on her pen and swung her foot over her knee, bouncing it. She noticed Peg grinning at the state of her loafers. "These are Alejandro's favorite," she told her. "Nice and battered, no sex appeal."

"Hey," said Peg, "I lived in Connecticut. I know about loafers. But since I moved down here, I've become quite attached to the fabulous array of slut shoes."

Kate eyed her dark brown stilettos. "If I took two steps in those, I'd fall and kill myself."

"No, you wouldn't," Peg said cheerfully. "You get used to them pretty fast. And they give you a built-in butt wiggle. Men love them."

Kate shuddered. "Where I come from, we don't approve of butt wiggle."

"And that's a crying shame," Alejandro's voice said behind her. He flashed his hypnotic white smile.

It shot into her bloodstream like a drug, making her heart speed. Her brain was inundated with images of a naked Alejandro under her, on top of her, behind her, next to her…murmuring hot, sexy words into her ear until she whimpered for release. Spinneys didn't whimper. Not ever. That was, by unwritten law, frowned upon even more than butt wiggle or tight spandex pants or thong bikinis. After all, Boston had been founded on tea, not sex.

Kate had a theory that the weather probably did have

a lot to do with it. As Marly said, it was hot down here. When settlers arrived in Florida, they'd probably almost died of heatstroke. When settlers had arrived on Plymouth Rock, they'd likely been frozen to the bone.

So the Mayflower crowd drank a lot of hot tea and bundled up by the fire. And the Miami crew, she figured, had gone skinny-dipping. There you had it: the evolution of culture.

"My neighbor would like Gracious back," Alejandro said, interrupting her train of thought.

"Oh. I was really enjoying her. But I guess she has to go home. Do you want me to bring her over to you later?"

"Yes, after we finish up here and we buy you some new shoes," he said, looking pointedly at her toes in the flapping loafer.

"How about a roll of clear packing tape instead? That'll fix the problem and they'll be good as new." She grinned up at him.

"No. Those were never good, and I'm not sure they were ever new, either. I think they've been passed down through your family for generations."

"Did I ask for your opinion on my footwear?"

"You did not. But I have clearly won the Flirt-Off, and the price you pay is new shoes of my choice, remember?"

"You have not won!"

"Flirt-Off?" Peggy and Marly said at the same time.

"I have definitely won. Come on, Kate, how can you even argue the point? Should I lay out all the details so that Peg and Marly can judge?"

"Details?" they asked, hopeful gleams in their eyes.

"No!" Kate glared at him.

"He is a Master Flirt," Marly told her. "He has to be. Look at what he does for a liv—" She jumped as Alejandro put his arm around her and squeezed, smiling broadly.

"I'm really at a loss as to why an accountant would need to flirt," Kate said, puzzled.

"So, what are all these notes about?" Alejo tweaked the yellow pad off her knee and examined it. He squinted. He turned it sideways. "What, were you a doctor in a past life? Or is this in a language I don't know?"

"Give me that," Kate said, annoyed. "So I flunked handwriting in first grade. I still got into Harvard."

"One word looked like demigod. Are you referring to me? Because there's nothing demi about Alejandro the Great, *mi amorcito*. You should know this by now."

*"Demographics,"* Kate said, through gritted teeth.

Peggy and Marly exchanged a glance. "You slept with him," they said. Peg added, "So he's definitely won the Flirt-Off."

"Wh—? I— That is *not* true."

"A gentleman doesn't kiss and tell," Alejandro murmured. "But I do see new shoes in your future today. Oh, yes, I do. I'm thinking snakeskin, five-inch heels, studded with rhinestones."

*"Value,"* said Kate, staring fixedly at the yellow pad, her face burning so hot that she was afraid her ears might blow off. "What does the After Hours customer value most? The service? The atmosphere? The price?"

"Yes," Alejandro mused. "Definitely rhinestones."

"Price isn't really a big consideration," Marly said.

"No rhinestones, sport."

Peggy nodded. "It's a toss-up between service and atmosphere."

"*Sport*," Alejo spat. "No. You will not call me that."

"Then you will not threaten me with rhinestones," Kate said sweetly. "Now, if you had to rank service or atmosphere higher, which would you pick?"

Marly tugged on her long dark braid. "Service," she finally said. "Especially Señor Maños." She winked at Peg.

Alejandro fell into a violent coughing fit.

"Señor what? What does that mean?" Kate tapped her pen on the legal pad.

"Mr. Hands."

"It's a product that we use in the course of a manicure or pedicure," Alejandro said smoothly. "Imported."

"Yes, from Peru," Peg added. "Fabulous. The clients can't get enough."

*Service,* Kate wrote down. *Superior products.* "And nobody else uses this?"

"No. We're unique when it comes to Señor Manos." Marly smiled.

"Great. Now, how do you set yourself apart from other salons?" Kate asked.

"Well, the fact that we're open until midnight, of course. And we serve wine and beer."

*Open till midnight,* Kate wrote. "Actually, I know of other salons and spas that serve wine, so you're not unique on that."

Peggy and Marly nodded. Alejandro was uncharacteristically quiet. He seemed annoyed with the two women; she didn't know why.

"You still with us, sport? Or are you taking a mental coffee break?"

He turned a malevolent gaze upon her. "*Purple* snakeskin," he said. "With a matching belt."

"Okay," Kate said briskly, ignoring him. "So then our conclusion is that in order to compete better in the salon and spa market, the one thing you guys can improve is your atmosphere. Correct?"

They all blinked at her. "We think our atmosphere is pretty cool," Marly said, gesturing around the place.

"Yeah," Peg backed her up. "Marly designed it all and did the floors and everything."

"The interior design is great," Kate told them. "Perfect for Miami. I'm not talking about any changes there. But you're pushing for a fun, sexy, almost night-club feel, right?"

They nodded.

"Then let's brainstorm how to push the envelope on that."

"*Okaaaay...*" They exchanged another glance and Kate had no problem reading their thoughts. What did Boston's Kate Spinney, in her baggy khakis, man's blue button-down and shredded loafers know about fun, or sex or hip nightclubs?

For the first time, she looked down at her clothes and found them lacking. Peg and Marly looked hip and sexy, each in her own different way. Peg wore stilettos, a short skirt and a form-fitting top. Marly wore two of those double cotton tank tops over a long peasant skirt. She didn't wear heels, but she did show a lot of glowing skin and some cleavage.

Kate felt like a small man next to them. She didn't like it at all. But purple snakeskin? She thought not. She steered her thoughts away from her appearance with a little leadership. "All right. When I say nightclub, what's the first thing that pops into each of your minds? Alejandro?"

"Shots."

"Peggy?"

"Strobe lights."

"Marly?"

"Loud synthesizer music."

Kate sighed. "None of those are going to work. Let's do adjectives now. Alejandro?"

"Tight, black, zippered."

"Peg?"

"Sexy."

"Marly?"

"Wild and crazy."

Kate nodded. "Okay, those are better. We can work with those." She chewed on the end of her pen for a moment. "You know, I think I can do a better job on a new marketing concept if I hang out here for a couple of days and just observe."

Alejandro frowned. "Oh, surely that's not necessary, Kate. You are a bright woman. You see the basics. I would hate for you to waste your time."

"It wouldn't be a waste," Kate told him. "I'd probably learn a lot and get some good ideas."

"What's to learn? Marly cuts hair. Peggy gives

massages. The, uh, nail techs do nails. It's as simple as that."

"Yes, but I could observe some of your clientele in action," Kate argued.

"Tell you what," Peg interrupted. "We're actually doing a private party next weekend, a customer appreciation night. Why don't you stop by then?"

Alejandro said quickly, "Kate would hate that."

Kate stared at him. "Excuse me, but Kate would like that very much, thanks."

"I just meant...well, that you don't have anything to wear. It'll be dressy and Miami-sexy. You can't show up in khaki pants and those loafers."

Kate folded her arms across her chest. "Well, I have it on the very best authority that I'm about to buy a pair of purple snakeskin stilettos. Am I not?"

"Er..."

"You know, Alejo, it's almost like you don't want me to come. What's up with that?"

"Of course I want you to come," he protested. "I just thought you might not be comfortable, that's all."

"Tell you what, sport. *I'll* make the decisions regarding my comfort, okay?"

*"No problema, sport."* He glared at her.

Marly tried to disguise a smile behind her hand, while Peggy just outright snickered.

"I'm so glad you find this entertaining," Alejandro snapped at them.

Kate capped her pen and stuck it in her pocket. "I'll continue to brainstorm." She elbowed her project partner. "And so will he." Kate undid the flap of her poor abused Hermès bag and shoved the yellow pad inside, to the detriment of both. She made it fit and then shut the purse again.

"But in the meantime, I've got some purple snakeskin pumps to buy with my fashion advisor, here."

# 13

*MIERDA, MIERDA, MIERDA!* Alejandro was going to knock his partners' heads together until they were flat on one side. How could they have done this to him? Kate couldn't come to the customer appreciation night! What were they smoking?

His cover would be completely blown. He'd be a laughingstock and Kate would never go out with him again. Not that he'd really taken her *out* yet. He needed to rectify that. But first, the shoes.

"I was teasing about the purple snakeskin, Kate," he said, as they left After Hours and walked out to the parking lot.

"I know." She headed straight for her car, which was, he guessed, the extremely dented, faded, blue 1970s Mercedes-Benz with the lacrosse stick in the rear window. "Where are you going?"

"I thought we were going to buy a pair of shoes?"

"We are. But I'll drive."

"I don't mind."

"I said I'll drive. This way."

"What's the matter, you don't like being driven by a woman?"

"That has nothing to do with it. I just happen to know where we're going." Actually, he *didn't* like being driven by a woman, but he knew it wasn't smart to admit that to her. He led her to his shiny black Porsche, and opened the door for her.

"My, my," Kate said, lifting a mocking eyebrow. "We do travel in style, don't we?"

Yet another reason for giving the damned pedicures. "Get into the car, Señorita Mercedes," he replied.

"That Mercedes was my grandmother's."

"Congratulations. But if you are waiting for me to apologize for driving a nice, new car, you will be waiting a very long time. Just because your money is old, Kate, does not make it better."

"I never meant—"

"Yes, *mi corazon,* you did." But he smiled at her to soften his words. "We are each from very different cultures. Yours may be understated, but that doesn't make mine wrong or bad. Here in Miami, expensive cars and jewelry are a reflection of prosperity, not bad taste."

Kate opened and then shut her mouth. Pleased that he'd reduced her to silence, he said, "Now, I am taking you to Miracle Mile, the fanciest shopping district in Coral Gables, if not Miami. So instead of groveling, you can lay waste to your wallet in the name of flashy, south Florida style!"

"Spinneys don't grovel," she said.

He burst out laughing. "Of course they don't. What was I thinking?"

"If you're going to mock me, you can just let me out at the next corner."

Alejandro hit the auto-lock button and cranked up the Brazilian song on the radio while he searched for parking. "No, Kate, you won't get away that easily. You're going to buy new shoes."

He found a spot near the most expensive shoe store on the street, parked and tugged out his unwilling passenger. Then he kissed her soundly, right on the curb, a most disgusting display of public affection.

Finally she pushed him off her. "No PDA!" she snapped.

He smirked. Of course a public display of affection would bother her. Holding tightly to her hand, he dragged her into the shoe boutique. When a pretty Latina salesgirl came forward, he said, "We would like to see high-heeled sandals in a size…?" He looked at Kate.

"Do they *have* to be high?"

"Yes."

"Seven and a half," she muttered, looking around her in dismay. "Oh, Christ. I'm in girlie hell. There are even matching purses here."

"Yes!" Alejandro said, eyeing her ragamuffin Hermès bag with disapproval.

"No," she said, clinging tight to it.

"You will have to buy an evening bag for the party," he said in severe tones.

"Why? Who needs an evening bag? I can't think of anything more useless."

"For your lipstick and compact, of course you must have one."

"I don't wear makeup."

"Your keys, then. And cellphone."

"I just shove those in my bra or a pocket."

Alejandro ignored her and seized an exquisite champagne-colored sandal with tiny rhinestones embedded in the four-inch heels. "This one," he told the salesgirl.

"That's not a shoe," Kate objected. "It's a piece of art."

Next he selected a bronze wedge-heeled sandal with an amber rhinestone on the toe. It was funky and cool and not at all her. She tried to explain that, but he flapped a hand at her.

A gorgeous, strappy, emerald-green metallic with silver lining joined the pile, followed by a black satin mule and a delicate pink kitten-heel.

"*Nooooo,*" Kate moaned. "Spinneys don't wear pink."

When he'd chosen about eighteen pairs of shoes for her, he made her sit down and roll her khaki pants to the knees.

The salesgirl took one incredulous look at Kate's loafers before she sat down and began the fitting process.

The champagne sandals were glorious on Kate, even though she couldn't walk in them. He took her arm as she wobbled awkwardly to the mirror. "See, I look ridiculous," she growled. "Like I borrowed the Queen's dancing shoes."

"They are beautiful on you," he said calmly.

"They're not! My toes stick out of them and look funny." She wiggled them.

"*Dios mio,* everyone's toes stick out of sandals! That is the whole point of them. It's far better for your toes to peek out of a sandal than out of the stitching on a mangled loafer."

"I can't walk in them."

"Practice. See, we're going to walk to the end of the boutique and back again. Put one foot in front of the other. Excellent…"

"My hips are swaying like a hooker's!" Kate complained. "I can't wear these. My family would faint." Then she stopped. Were fainting Spinneys necessarily a bad thing? Wasn't she becoming Just Kate? Hmm…

"We'll take them," Alejandro told the salesgirl.

But before making her final decision, Kate made an unsteady leap for the box and checked the price tag. "Holy Mother of God! I'm not paying six hundred dollars for a pair of sandals."

"You are," Alejandro said. "You won't feel a thing, I promise. Are fantastically wealthy shampoo heiresses always this cheap?"

"I'm not cheap! I'm frugal."

"Not today, you're not. Now be quiet and try on the wedges."

"Wow, these are actually comfy," Kate said in shocked tones, once she had them on her feet. "Amazing."

"*Sí, señorita.*" The salesgirl smiled at her. "And they are lovely with either skirts or trousers." She stared fixedly at Kate's baggy, shapeless pants and said no more.

"But I don't know if I can get used to metallic shoes or those little tie things around the ankles."

"You can," Alejandro assured her. "We'll take them. And look, Kate, they are only three hundred and eighty-five dollars. A big savings!"

She turned green.

"Now for the black suede peep-toe pumps." He pulled the box over and handed one to her.

"I'd only wear those for funerals."

"Nonsense! These are everyday shoes. You wear them with jeans and a studded black belt and a nice big hobo bag."

"Spinneys don't wear black in the daytime."

Alejandro pretended to smack her. "You know, for someone who was so eager to be free of her family, you seem to like their rules a lot."

She frowned. Savagely, she thrust her feet into the black peep-toes. She took a few steps in them and cocked a hip in front of the mirror. "Fine. I'll take them." She looked at the salesgirl. "And do you have a belt?"

"*Sí, señorita.* I have the perfect belt." She returned with a monster black suede belt studded with hardware. The thing even cinched with a faux padlock.

Kate stared at it as if it were a poisonous toad. She shut her eyes. "How do you wear that? I mean, what do you wear it with?"

"*Señorita,* you let me call them at shop across the street. I have them bring you some nice stretch jeans and tops, okay?"

"*Sí,*" Alejandro told her. "That would be wonderful. *Gracias.*"

"Did she say *stretch?*" Kate asked faintly.

"Yes."

"But Spin—"

"To hell with what the Spinneys do! Are you your own woman, or are you a paper doll who takes orders from some unwritten WASP code?"

She seemed to be staring at the gold chain around his neck. She looked repelled by it. Finally she blinked and looked away. "I'm…my own woman," she said. "And I'm in Miami now, not Boston."

"Good." He seized her and kissed her thoroughly once again. Once again, she pushed him away.

"I'm my own woman, but I don't like PDA!"

Alejandro threw up his hands. "We're not in public."

"No, we're only on a security video, that's all."

The door of the boutique across the street opened and a tiny blonde staggered over with an armload of clothing.

She looked in disbelief at what Kate was wearing and shook her head. In rapid-fire Spanish, she delivered a fashion monologue of which Kate didn't understand a word. Then the two salesgirls dragged her into the stockroom, since there was no dressing room in the shoe boutique.

"Help!" Kate mouthed at Alejandro. He just waved goodbye to her and grinned. Then he relaxed in one of two leather chairs that were obviously there for the miserable men dragged in by their women. He took a little snooze.

*"Mira, mira, señor!"* A few minutes later, their original salesgirl clapped her hands and he opened his eyes to see the new Kate. His jaw went slack.

The new Kate wore long, faded stretch jeans with a little Chinese embroidery on one leg, plus the peep-toed skyscraper heels, a tiny, tight, black belly shirt and the black belt with all the hardware. They'd also decked her out in a wide silver cuff bracelet, modern silver earrings and a warm, cinnamon lipstick that brought out the green of her eyes and the red in her crazy, wiry hair. This they'd pinned back on one side with a rhinestone-studded barrette.

She looked stunning. She looked smokin' hot. She looked like the kind of chick who rode a Harley, delighted in cruelty to men and smoked a cigar while gambling the night away. Best of all, she didn't look in the least bit available or cheap. Just plain sexy.

"K-Kate?" he said.

"Yup." She still wobbled a little in the shoes, but the blonde from across the street said, "*Mira, señorita.* You extend your leg, like so. You use the heel for grace and for height, eh? It is not to be stumbled upon. Find your center of balance, yes? Then take even, smooth strides. *Sí! Perfecto.* You walk with me." She took Kate's arm and they sashayed down the length of the store and then sashayed back.

*Dios mio,* the sight of Kate dressed like this was killing him. He wanted to throw her on the floor of the boutique and have his way with her, right that instant.

He restrained himself. "We'll take everything," he said.

Kate raised her eyebrows at him. "Oh we will, will we? You're mighty free with my wallet, sport."

"Somebody has to be." He remained unperturbed, turning to the salesgirls. "Now, what else have you got?"

"Hey! I'm not buying any more than this. This is bad enough—it's the equivalent of the average mortgage payment."

"Kate, you've agreed to buy several different pairs of shoes, so you need more than one pair of jeans and a shirt to go with them. Or are you going to wear those fabulous sandals with your Brooks Brothers' men's gear?"

The salesgirls hustled her off to the back again, Kate muttering and complaining the whole way.

This time, when they returned with her, she wore a bronze lamb-leather miniskirt with a skin-tight chocolate tank, no bra, and chocolate suede platform heels. They'd put gold dangly earrings on her, and a four-inch wide gold mesh bracelet encircled one thin wrist.

Alejandro had to pick carpet fibers off his tongue after it dragged on the floor, especially since this time Kate vamped playfully in front of the mirror and slapped her tush for him.

The salesgirls giggled. "*Esta caliente,* no?"

He finally found his voice. "She'll wear that one out when we leave."

"No, sport, I'll wear *you* out." Kate sent him a smoldering look and actually tossed her hair at him.

The girls hauled her off to the back again, and she reappeared in a deep emerald-green velvet cocktail dress with an asymmetrical hemline that bared one knee but covered the other leg to mid-calf. Her skin glowed ivory against it, and they'd lined her eyes so they looked darker and more mysterious. The neckline of the dress was the showstopper, though: it plunged in a deep V to the top of her waist, held together under her breasts by only a copper filigree pin. She wore the metallic green strappy sandals with it, and they'd found a tiny bronze evening bag for her.

Alejandro took a deep breath. "You look like a goddess," he said simply.

She flushed and fiddled with the bag before meeting his gaze again. "No need to go overboard, A. I'm just playing dress-up."

"I'll buy that one for her, with the shoes and bag," he said to the salesgirls. "Will you wrap that up separately?"

"Alejandro, you can't—do you know how much this—*no*. You are most certainly not buying this outfit for me. I forbid you."

"Pay no attention to her," he said, digging out his wallet and producing a credit card. So it would take months to pay it off—who cared? She looked like a young empress. To him, it was imperative that she have the dress.

"You know, sport, you really tick me off sometimes!" Kate said dangerously. "I can't accept that from you. It's not right. And I'm tired of being ordered around." She turned to the salesgirls. "Let me make this clear to you. You swipe his card, and I won't buy any of the rest of it. You add those items to *my* tab. Understand?"

They blinked at her. They looked at him. They looked at each other. They mentally totaled up the thousands of dollars being spent in their respective stores. And they did as she told them.

Alejandro's blood boiled. It wasn't that he blamed the girls. He blamed Kate. "You won't allow me to give you a gift?" He asked the question in deceptively calm tones.

"Alejo, it's too much."

"Isn't that for me to decide, not you?"

"No. It's one thing to buy me a scarf or a silver bracelet. But this—it's just not right."

"Ah. The heiress won't accept a present from the peasant. Why, because you might feel obligated?"

"Stop it! This has nothing to do with that."

"This is your once-in-a-lifetime fling with a man who wears a gold chain around his neck, eh? Better keep it casual. I'm just your cheap hunk, a low-class boy toy, a temporary pet. You wouldn't want to owe me anything."

"What?" Kate looked shaken. "What are you talking about? I don't think of you as a pet!"

"Oh, so you're serious about this relationship?"

"Serious? We don't even know each other that well!"

His anger and hurt grew. "That's what I thought."

"Alejandro, you're not being reasonable—"

He glowered down at her from his superior height. "Oh, but I'm *Latin,* remember? We're not supposed to be reasonable. According to your WASP stereotypes, we're hotheads, so I wouldn't want to disappoint you." He opened the shop's door and stalked out.

Through the corner of his eye, he saw Kate dig a credit card out of her scuffed wallet and hand it to the salesgirls. Then she followed him outside.

"Don't put Wendell's words into my mouth!"

"Same family. Same attitude."

"That's so unfair! What is your problem?" she shouted.

"I don't have a problem," he retorted.

"Yes, you do. You're full of attitude right now, just because I won't let you buy me something. You are so…" She searched for words. "You're *over the top!* It's like you don't know boundaries or limits. You're too big, and you're too gorgeous and you're too persuasive. You're too good a lover, and you're too macho and you're just *too much!*"

He just stared at her, the crazy woman. She stood there in the green velvet dress with only one shoe on, her hair flying every which way. Sparks shot from her eyes and spots of red burned high on those miraculous cheek-bones. She was furious and he didn't understand why.

"New Englanders *are* understated, and we don't like taking extravagant gifts. I won't apologize for it! You, on the other hand—you're like a tall, dark, handsome *steamroller.* I have one lousy cup of coffee with you and before I know it I have a pig, and a screaming orgasm and a leather miniskirt! You're just…out of control."

Alejandro grabbed her by the shoulders and kissed her roughly. Then he said, "That's a load of *mierda.* You're just upset because *you're* too *under* control." And then he turned on his heel and walked away.

# 14

*I AM NOT too under control! I'm engaged in releasing
my inner rebel. I just don't always know where to start.*
Kate looked at all the shopping bags rattling against her
in the back of a cab and felt ill. *I bought all this fancy
stuff, didn't I? I left Boston and moved all the way down
here by myself. I have a pig in my condo. I am working
on being Just Kate. And when I get up the nerve, I will
dance on that damned table, too. It just has to be the
right time and place.*

Alejandro was a jerk. He'd walked away and left her
by herself in retail hell, hadn't he? In the company of
those tiny, bosomy creatures who would look chic and
sexy even if garbed in white kitchen trash bags with
banana peels on their heads.

He'd abandoned her to their evildoing, which
included dragging her to the custom cosmetics place
next door, of all things! Yet another tiny, bosomy
creature on spindly heels had chattered at her rapidly
in Spanish while she custom-blended gook in a bottle
for her face. Then she'd attacked her with it, as well as
with various brushes, vials and pencils. She'd smeared
colors not found in nature onto Kate's face and charged

her close to four hundred dollars for a whole bag of makeup that she would never remember how to use.

By the time Kate had staggered in her new clothes and new face to the waiting taxi, she was shell-shocked. The three tiny *señoritas* smiled and waved, having had the time of their lives. Kate just felt exhausted.

She picked up her car and drove home, horrified when a trucker honked his horn at her and a college kid in the lane next to her whistled and then waggled his tongue between two fingers. "Sicko!" she yelled.

When she arrived at her condo she waved at old Mr. Landry, who lived on her floor, and bent into the back of the Mercedes to fish out her shopping bags.

She heard a sickening crunch of metal on metal and pulled her head out to find that old Mr. Landry had driven his Bonneville right into another parked car.

Kate tottered over on her high heels to make sure he was okay. He glared at her, his lazy eye rolling up into its socket. "Get away from me. This is your fault, missy!"

She gaped at him. "*My* fault?"

"All gussied up like a five-hunnert-dollar hooker. What's a man to do, huh? Mincing around, a-lookin' like you kin suck a golf ball through a garden hose—"

"*Mister Landry!*"

"Your fault, I'm a-tellin' you."

"Tell that to your insurance company."

"I will!"

She gaped at him. "Don't you ever speak to me again, you disgusting old fart." Kate whirled and stalked back to her car. *Unbelievable.*

Laden with her shopping bags, she stormed the main

door of her building in her high heels and tottered past the concierge desk. The uniformed attendant behind it called out. "Madam? I'm sorry but you'll need to check in here, please."

She turned to face him. "Kevin, I live here."

"M-Miss Spuh—Spinney?" He stared. "Is that you?"

"In the belly-shirted flesh." She grinned.

*"Wow."*

"Thanks, I think." She turned and continued to lug her bags toward the elevators.

"Uh, Miss Spinney? I hate to even ask you this, but there was a complaint lodged from your own phone number about you. Something about a pig?"

She stopped and turned her head. "Oh, Kevin." She laughed. "A pig? In my unit? Don't be ridiculous."

"Yes, ma'am."

After her brief elevator ride, Kate stumbled into her condo and dumped all of her bags. Gracious came out immediately, squealing and grunting and bouncing up and down on her stubby front legs. Kate looked at her sadly and dropped to the floor to kiss her little snout. "I'm going to miss you."

"Oh, how touching," Wendell said, emerging from the guestroom with his signature smirk. It faded immediately, to be replaced by a look of horror when he saw her face and new clothes. "Katydid? Is that you under there, or has J Lo taken over your body?"

Kate stood up and put her hands on her hips. "Like it? This is the new me."

His lip curled. "You look like South Beach trash."

She should have known better than to expect a

positive reaction, but she was hurt anyway. "Pretty expensive trash."

He shrugged. "Whatever the budget, you're channeling 'available.' Grandfather Spinney and Aunt Cornelia would have a coronary if they saw you like that."

"Like what? In clothes that fit?"

"Those don't just fit, Katy. They display your goods like they're in a shop window."

"Why is that such a crime? I'm not even thirty."

"Did your Latin stallion put you up to this? What's next? Bleached hair, double-E knockers and lips the size of a pool raft?"

"Why do you have to be so hateful all the time, Wendell?" She turned away from him and got Gracious a couple of grapes out of the refrigerator.

He had the nerve to look offended. "Hateful? I'll tell you what's hateful—letting your greasy pimp of a sex toy throw your own flesh and blood out of your home. Choosing him over me."

Her jaw dropped open and she had to take a moment to compose herself. "Wendell, I didn't do any such thing. You pushed Alejandro—and me—to the limits of human tolerance. If he hadn't removed you, I would have. And stop calling him rude names."

"What's *hateful*," Wendell continued as if he hadn't heard her, "is forcing a family member to live with a disease-carrying, flea-ridden slab of walking bacon." He eyed Gracious with malevolence. "Speaking of her, you owe me four grand."

"What? Why?"

"That F-ing barnyard animal pissed in my suitcase!"

Kate put a hand up to her mouth.

"It soaked my suit, my folded custom shirts, my handmade shoes, my extra set of Pratesi sheets, and quite a few other things."

She bit back a wild cheer.

"And don't tell me to wash them and forget about it. I'm not wearing pig pee, and I'm not sleeping in it, either. So unless you want your little antics with the greaseball broadcast to the board and the family, you'll be sitting down right now to write me a check."

*Like hell!* Fury engulfed her, and she couldn't even speak to him. Kate scooped up Gracious and stalked to her bedroom, then slammed the door.

In private, she gave the pig a dazzling smile and danced across the room with her. She kissed the top of her fuzzy porcine head. "So *that's* why you didn't need to go out that night. *Good job,* Miss Piggy! You go, girl. Or, uh, I guess you went."

The pig squealed, and Kate gave her three more grapes and a dried apricot from a bowl on her dresser. She thought about how much she did not want to give Gracious back to her owner. She sighed and kicked off the infernal black peep-toe heels.

Alejandro was not a jerk. If not for him, she'd never have met Gracious. And he was a saint in comparison to Wendell.

When she heard the door slam, she assumed that her cousin had left her in peace for the time being. She fantasized about calling the police to remove him permanently...but even though he was obnoxious, black-mailing scum, he was family. She didn't think she could actually call the cops on him.

She padded around her condo gathering the pig's things. She hauled the bags of food and litter down to her car first, casting a look of dislike at old Mr. Perv-Pants, who was arguing with a police officer and the owner of the parked car he'd run into. She popped her trunk and dumped the supplies into it. She was closing the trunk when Landry said, "There she is, right there. Now you look at that ass and tell me you wouldn't-a wrecked yourself, officer."

*Christ Almighty.* Kate pushed her sunglasses farther up her nose and ignored them as both men turned to stare at her. She walked calmly back into the building, but not before she heard the officer say, "I certainly see your point, sir."

*Maybe I* should *go back to my baggy khakis!* Kate was torn between outrage, amusement and utter embarrassment. But it was also just a tiny bit thrilling to have caused an accident, even for a nasty old geezer with a freaky eye and a toilet mouth. She'd definitely never caused an accident before. Kate treated them to an extra little wiggle before she disappeared into the freight elevator. *Kiss it, boys.*

She decided to wait half an hour before bringing out Gracious, so that old Mr. Landry would be gone. Kate turned on the radio and found some salsa music. Then she dragged her shopping bags into her bedroom and put her new things away in the closet.

She looked at herself in a mirror, twisting her mouth.

Screw Wendell. She looked great, if she did say so herself, but she didn't look like *her*.

The custom cosmetics girl had applied her new makeup with a trowel, and giving in to her Boston up-bringing, Kate blotted off half the lipstick. Then she stared at her eyes. They looked huge, dark and myste-rious, but they also reminded her uncomfortably of those camouflage fatigues that troops wore in combat. Gray, olive, brown and army-green. And she wore so much mascara that it was a miracle she could blink.

It had to come off. Kate stripped out of the belly shirt and the stretch jeans, and turned on the shower in her bathroom. "C'mon, Gracious!" she called. "Time for a bath. I can't return you smelly, and I have it on the best authority that I look like South Beach trash or a 'five-hunnert-dollar hooker.'"

Once Kate had washed them both, dried them both and applied a little less makeup to the best of her ability, she called Alejandro's house. "Rude Yankee, here. Today, you get a free pig if you'll buy an apology."

After a pause he laughed, and she sagged in relief. She'd refused to acknowledge how much his anger had bothered her.

"I should apologize first, Kate," he said. "I can be a little hardheaded at times."

"Hey, you have to wait your turn, sport. I get to sell you on mine first."

He chuckled. "Okay. What model and make of apology? What are the special features? Do they include dinner and dancing? Complimentary thong panties?"

Damn. That was the one thing she'd forgotten to

buy. You couldn't wear big cotton underpants with anything she'd bought today, that was for sure. However…Spinneys didn't wear butt floss. It just wasn't done.

"The apology might encompass dinner, but the thong is not included. Dancing is negotiable."

Alejandro sighed. "I don't know about this. You were awfully cruel to me, and all I did was try to buy you an outfit."

"You drove off and *left* me, sport. With two beautiful Columbian sadists who clearly understood the meaning of *shampoo heiress,* and milked it to the limit. My credit card company has already called to ask about the break in spending patterns. I believe they thought that some criminal mastermind was outfitting his entire harem."

"I dunno," he mused. "I'm still feeling awfully mistreated."

"They dragged me to a custom cosmetics establishment where they made my face look like a freakin' *color wheel.* And don't forget about the free pig. You are going to accept this apology or I will jam it down your throat with my scruffy old loafers, got that?"

"Kate, *mi corazon.* May I offer a piece of unsolicited advice?"

She sighed. "Oh, please. I'm sure I couldn't possibly live without it."

"You should never apply for a job with the United Nations, or accept a post as ambassador to anywhere. You have no tact or finesse."

"Thank you. Now can I bring the pig over, or not?"

"I will welcome you, the pig and the apology with open arms," Alejandro said. "But…I am still lobbying for the thong."

AN HOUR LATER, after a brief stop back at Miracle Mile at a boutique that sold a bottomless variety of butt floss, bras, lacy teddies and naughty nighties, Kate parked her Mercedes outside Alejandro's small, neat house in Coconut Grove.

Her new Brazilian lace thingie—what the hell was it called? A tanga?—had wedged itself right where she didn't want it, and something in the matching apricot lace bra was digging into her spine.

She got out of the car and let Gracious out, too, scratching her on the head. "The way that horrid woman acted when I brought you into the shop! It's not like you're a cockroach, now is it, baby?"

Gracious squealed and dug her snout into the grass.

"Can you believe I had to swear to spend a thousand dollars in there just so she would let you stay? What was I supposed to do, let you suffocate in the car? And now I have butt floss in every color." She hoped her inner rebel was happy, because Just Kate was actively afraid of blisters where the sun didn't shine.

She stomped as well as she could—it was, admittedly, hard to stomp in four-inch heels—onto Alejandro's porch and hammered on the door.

"Do I look like trash? Like I could suck a golf ball through a garden hose?" she demanded when he opened the door.

He blinked. "I beg your pardon? *What* did you say?"

He stood there barefoot, in jeans and an open white shirt. "And what did you do to your eyes?" He began to laugh.

"What do you mean, what did I do to my eyes? I used makeup. I lined them and used shadow like the girl said I was supposed to," she said crossly. "And an old pervert in my parking lot had an accident with a parked car. He says it was because of me, that I looked like I could suck a—"

Alejandro pursed his lips and cocked his head at her.

"—golf ball through a garden hose."

He shook his head. "Maybe a jelly bean," he said. "Or a Tic Tac. Only the best of professionals could attempt the legendary golf ball."

"He said I looked like a pro! Like a five-hundred-dollar hooker. And it's all thanks to *you*."

"How old was this guy?"

"At least eighty."

"Then that was a true compliment," Alejandro noted, "since rates have skyrocketed since his time. I'd say personally that if we fixed your eye makeup, you could be a two-thousand-dollar hooker."

"Really?" Kate's eyes widened. Then she glared at him. "Why did I consider that a compliment, even for a moment? You have a very strange effect on me, Torres."

He grinned and took Gracious's leash from her. "So here's my bonus pig. Where's my apology?"

"You don't get one now, since you insulted me."

He sighed mournfully. "I didn't. I just explained to you that it's a compliment."

"No, you're saying I look cheap!"

Alejandro's eyes widened. "You think two thousand dollars is cheap? Oh. Well, you *are* a shampoo heiress. I forgot."

*"Gaaaaaah!"*

"Care for a drink?"

"Yes. I think it's the only way I can tolerate you." She looked around her, at Alejandro's things and his decor. He had a modern brown leather couch set into a steel frame, lots of plants that he actually kept alive, and a huge magical-realist painting on one wall.

It depicted a woman and a boy on a flying rag rug, while another woman in a pink smock sucked them towards her with a hairdryer. She stood outside of a house, the door open behind her and filled with cheerful yellow.

Alejo saw Kate looking at it and smiled. "Tia Carlotta, my mother and me after my father died. The Gabriel Garcia Márquez version of us, anyway."

Kate felt the oddest urge to walk into the painting. She couldn't understand it. "What's the symbolism of the hairdryer? And why does it operate in reverse?"

"Tia Carlotta and my mother started a beauty salon after my father passed on," Alejandro said quietly. "I used to help there after school and on Saturdays. In the painting, Tia summons us with the hairdryer. Toward a new life."

"I love the whimsical style."

"I am glad you like it. That painting will always hang somewhere in my home and in my heart."

Kate looked around some more. The floor was a pale, neutral tile, with Peruvian woven rugs here and there. A large fountain played softly in one corner.

She followed him into the kitchen, which was modernized with stainless steel appliances. But a large stone mortar and pestle dominated one counter, the ancient tools incongruous among all the shiny machines.

Alejandro made her a drink called a mojito, which was made with crushed mint leaves, about a pound of sugar and a great deal of rum. One sip of it and her eyeballs did figure eights in her head.

He laughed. "That will get you in the mood for dinner and dancing later."

"Later? It's already eight o'clock."

"Kate, *mi corazon,* you are in Miami. We won't even have appetizers until 11:00, we'll dine around midnight and we'll stay out until at least 4:00 a.m."

She gaped at him. "But I'm starving! And I'll be asleep by 11:00."

"If you're hungry I will grill some chorizo and heat a tamal for you."

"What are those? Are they animal or vegetable?"

"Chorizo is a sausage and a tamal is similar to a Mexican tamale, but much larger and with slightly different ingredients. You may have both with *ahi,* a hot sauce."

Alejandro prepared the food, and Kate ate it with pleasure, all before 8:45 p.m. She finished her mojito and looked around for more.

"No, Kate, I think you'd better switch to water or you'll pass out on me."

She frowned at him. "I can handle my liquor. Besides, what are we going to do for two hours, meditate?"

His eyes deepened, and suddenly she knew exactly what he wanted to do for two hours.

"That's supposed to happen after the date," she argued.

"Is that another unwritten WASP rule?" Alejandro asked, the gold chain around his neck gleaming in the low lighting. "Spinneys only do it after dinner? Because if so, it's a rule that I think we should break."

# 15

ALEJANDRO MOVED TOWARD KATE, still unable to believe how sexy she looked in the jeans, belly shirt, bad-girl belt and heels. But especially endearing was the fact that she'd somehow gotten black smudges and dots—probably mascara—all over the shadow on one eye, and slipped a bit with the liner on the other.

She was utterly incompetent in the beauty arena, but for some reason this made Alejo want to kiss her all over. So he started to do just that. Then he shrugged out of his shirt and took her onto his lap on the couch and told her in Spanish all the dirty-sweet things he was going to do to her.

*I'm going to caress every inch of you with my hands and my mouth. I'm going to suck your nipples through your little cotton shirt until you beg me to rip it off you.*

*Then I'm going to touch your ass through your jeans and walk my fingers down between your legs until you moan and push against them, trying to find relief.*

*I'm going to push you onto your back and peel off your jeans. Spread your legs and put my mouth right there and lick you through your panties.*

*Then I'm going to take the rest of your clothes off and*

*bend you over the back of the couch while I play with your breasts and take you from behind. I'm going to drive you hard and wet until you scream my name and I'm burned into you erotically like a brand....*

He knew she didn't understand a word he was saying, but she definitely comprehended his intent, as he stripped the studded black belt off of her and nuzzled at her breasts, stroking the peaks into hot little pebbles. He bit her through the black belly T, and she gasped, arching her back to give him better access.

He made twin wet spots on the black T, and then treated her belly button to a sensual invasion, licking into it and around it, stabbing his tongue below the waistband of her jeans.

Then he tugged the shirt over her head, growling his pleasure when he saw the whisper-thin, apricot lace bra. He left it on, scraping his teeth against her nipples this time and seeming to excite her even more.

He plunged his hands down the back of her jeans, taking full advantage of the stretchy fabric, and encountered bare flesh...with just a tiny bit of lace at the top. Could it be? Had she bought, just for him, a thong?

He was already hard, but just the possibility took him to cold steel. "What have you got on, *mi amor?* Hmm?" He didn't give her time to reply, just stood her on her feet and yanked the new jeans all the way down her legs. She stepped out of them, now wearing only her lingerie, her high heels and a wicked smile. She turned so that her bottom faced him, looked back at him over her shoulder, and tucked her hair behind her ear.

He almost had a coronary. Instead of the serviceable

white cotton underpants she'd had on at her condo, Kate wore an apricot lace *tanga* that matched her bra. And it was just as whisper-thin.

It rode the curves of her cheeks, half impudence and half innocence. About midway down, it disappeared into the dusky crevice between them.

Maybe it was the new lingerie, or maybe it was the mojito, but something sure had gotten into Kate because she bent over a little and wagged her bottom at him like a naughty showgirl.

His voice ragged, he asked, "Do they teach you to do that in cotillion class?" Then he sprang at her, intent on dragging her down for all kinds of nefarious purposes.

But she twisted away, escaping into his kitchen in search of more mojitos. He went after her and caught her with her head in the refrigerator, where he'd stuck the pitcher.

Alejandro hooked her by the tanga and pulled her out, pitcher and all.

"Hey! You just ruined a perfectly good permanent wedgie," she said. "I was starting to dig it."

"Are you sure you want more to drink?"

"Do I look like I'm waffling?" she asked, raising the pitcher.

He shrugged and found her glass. She poured out a healthy amount and then handed the pitcher back to him. He filled his own glass. "Cheers." *Clink.*

Kate took a big swallow and stared down at herself. "I feel so silly, like I'm impersonating somebody else." Her expression was part mocking, part wistful.

He reached out a hand to stroke her cheek. "You're not impersonating anyone. You're just discovering a new side of Kate. The sexy side. Your inner vamp." Was she actually blushing in the dim light?

"I like both sides," Alejandro added. "Remember, I chased after Khaki Kate, too. Even her orphaned toes were some hot little piggies."

"Yeah, and look at her now. Khaki Kate is wearing butt floss." She sucked down some more mojito. "But I'll tell you a secret. Butt floss is not really that uncomfortable. I can't believe it! Though I will say that it would be a serious bummer for anyone with hemorrhoids."

Alejandro shuddered. "Let's not go there, *mi corazon.*"

"Yeah, let's not."

"Come with me." He took her hand and led her into his bedroom, where he lit a big pillar candle and then sat on the edge of his platform bed. "Give me your foot."

He unfastened her sandal and ran his hands up her beautiful, lean calves, massaging and appreciating the muscle he found there. "Now the other."

She gave him her other foot and he removed that sandal, too. Then he turned her and pulled her into his lap so that his stomach nudged her spine and his cock nestled under her rear. He wrapped his arms around her and kissed the back of her neck, her thin shoulders, several vertebrae.

He stroked her waist and belly, her rib cage, her arms, her thighs. He covered her breasts with his palms and warmed them, massaged them, brought them back to being stiff little peaks.

He unhooked her bra and slid the straps down her arms, tossing it aside so that he could feel her naked flesh. He took his time and savored her.

Only then did he slide his hands back down to her thighs and inward, higher. She quivered in his arms as his fingers approached her mons, and she stiffened with tension as he cupped it, stroked it, slid the tanga to one side.

Her crazy, curly hair tickled his chin as she arched her back, and he inhaled the familiar scent of her shampoo as he parted her folds and searched for ways to bring her pleasure. What he was doing had her twining her feet around his calves and moaning softly, which was always a good sign. He slid a finger deep inside her and found her clitoris with his thumb, moving it in slow, slick circles while her feet abraded the hair on his calves and her breathing came more quickly.

"You like that, *mi amor?*"

"Yes," she whispered, moving restlessly against him.

He settled his chin over her shoulder so that he could watch his fingers bring her pleasure. He was beyond hard now, aching with the need to plunge inside her, but he forced himself to remain patient and heat her slowly to the boiling point. There was a time for fast and furious, but this was not it.

Kate's breath came in shallow gasps now, and she was beyond wet as he played her with every instinct he had. With a hoarse cry, she bucked against his hand, threw her head back and quivered uncontrollably in his arms.

Knowing that he'd pleased her, he felt an intense satisfaction that was almost greater than reaching climax himself. Alejandro finally tipped her forward a little and entered her, exhilarated as she made another soft moan of pleasure. She still wore the tanga and the sight of it, too, turned him on.

He gripped her hips and moved inside her, feeling that he could die a happy man in the tight, wet heat of her. But the angle was difficult for her, so he lay back on the bed and moved into the center of the mattress, tugging her with him.

"Now, straddle me," he told her.

"But…shouldn't I turn around?"

"No." He ran his hands over the smooth, soft skin of her bottom. "Lean forward."

"Alejo, I can't!"

"Why?"

"Because…because I'm sticking my ass in your face!" She seemed mortified.

He laughed. "Not exactly. But we can do that, if you prefer." He began to pull her toward him, with evil intent.

"No! No, no, no. We are *not* doing that."

"Then take off your panties and straddle me. I happen to like your rear view, Kate."

She looked at him dubiously, but slid out of the tanga and dropped it on the floor so that she was entirely naked. Then she climbed onto him, awkwardly. "This just doesn't feel right," she complained.

"Lean forward onto your knees, *mi amor*." As she did so, Alejandro almost had another coronary; the sight was so erotic. He parted her and slid in, pulled her back onto him inch by delicious inch.

*"Ooooh,"* she breathed.

Transfixed by sensation and the visual, he couldn't even speak. He just moved his hips, pumping in and out of her and tried not to go crazy and hurt her.

Then Kate began to move her bottom in a circle, changing the pressure and the angle as he drove in and out. He lost control and lost his grip on reality, too, as every nerve in his body seemed to zip down to his cock and join the party.

"Deeper," Kate coaxed, and upped the tempo. "Faster. Please…"

He was only too happy to oblige, slamming into her, afraid he was being too rough. "I do not want to hurt you," he said.

Kate shook her head. "You're not…feels so good… like I'm melting all over you." She caught her breath and pushed back, gripping him with her inner muscles. Then she caressed the root of him as he slid out of her, touching his *huevos* as he slid in.

He didn't know where the shout came from, but it emerged from his own throat, just as he exploded within her, the pleasure so intense that it was almost pain. He sat up, wrapping his arms around her as if he'd never let her go, and spilled himself inside her in the most intense climax he'd ever had.

She collapsed against him, breathing hard, but he didn't think she'd come a second time, and this bothered him. Alejo cupped her breasts, nuzzled her neck and moved softly inside her as he plucked at her nipples.

He actually felt the wave of her orgasm as it crested over her and shook her gently—an amazing, deeply intimate experience that he'd never had. It triggered a gentle aftershock of his own, creating eddies that moved in concentric circles, all the way to his heart.

# 16

THREE HOURS LATER, Kate sipped at another mojito in a Brazilian restaurant that Alejandro had taken her to. With a feeling of unreality, she watched the girls dancing on the bar in their tiny skirts with plenty of cheeky cheek hanging out.

It was cheeky cheek clad in fishnet tights, cheeky cheek decorated with thongs in various colors and cheeky cheek displayed with garters and thigh-high stockings.

Alejandro laughed at her expression and squeezed her shoulders. "They don't do this in Cape Cod, eh?"

Kate shook her head emphatically. "No, they do not." She took another sip of her mojito, transfixed by all the sassy little asses up there, gyrating and wiggling like ripe, tempting fruit.

She looked around at the men in the restaurant, all of whom looked highly appreciative of the entertainment. "You could feed these guys Alpo and they'd never notice. I bet all of them walk out of here with the worst cricks in their necks."

"Ah, but the food and drink are so good that they don't mind." Alejandro winked at her. "Besides, I think you're in for an unexpected treat, *mi corazon*. It's not only the men who get sore necks."

And sure enough, when the music stopped the three Brazilian girls were helped down from the bar by some very handsome young men, all of whom swung themselves up onto the bar and began a most interesting dance of their own.

Kate's chin dropped onto the straw in her drink, leaving a circular indentation that she'd probably have for the next couple of days. Chippendales had nothing on these guys! They were smoking hot. Two of them looked like they could bench-press Volkswagen Beetles for hours, while the one in the middle had butt and thigh muscles that were beyond drool-worthy. In fact, Kate had never seen a man who could do such things with his pelvis! He swiveled, he thrust, he grinned suggestively…and he did it all in perfect time to the dance music.

Women all over the restaurant began clapping and yelling encouragement, hooting and egging him on. The dancers managed to be far more erotic than any stripper Kate had seen at a bachelorette party—without taking anything off.

Her initial shock faded into delight. There was no sleaziness, no cheesiness. Just three men up there having the time of their lives performing for women. Okay, so they had hot sweaty chests—one of them wore an open vest, the others tight T-shirts. And their pants were certainly not baggy.

"Kate, you want to get up there with them and shake it?" Alejandro teased.

*Yes.* "Absolutely not. I've got a great view right here."
She wasn't ready to share her silly goal with Alejandro.

"You mean Spinneys don't dance on bars, either?"

*Hell, no! Which is why I want to. But I'm not drunk
enough.* She stuck her tongue out at him. Of course, his
response was to chase it into her mouth and recapture
it with his teeth. She fell headlong into Alejandro's kiss,
wrapping her arms around him and not even protesting
when he pulled her off her bar stool and onto his lap.

He tasted sweet, of mint and rum—and spicy as well,
from the remnants of the *ahi* sauce. She could feel his
arousal pressing against her bottom, and it sent a flash
of heat through her. She pulled back from his mouth and
whispered, "You're insatiable!"

He nodded, his teeth flashing white in the low
lighting. "Yes, for you, *mi corazon.*" The gold chain
around his neck gleamed, and she reached out a finger
to touch it. She disapproved of it, as she did of any
jewelry on men, but it gave him a dangerous, exotic look.

"I know you hate it, Kate."

She met his gaze ruefully.

"But I'll never take it off. It was a gift from my
mother."

She tried to imagine her own mother giving any man
a gold chain, and giggled helplessly. She never giggled,
and it embarrassed her. Then again, she never kissed
men in public, and she certainly never sat in their laps
in restaurants. What was happening to her? Her inner
rebel was going nuts.

"Why is that funny?" Alejo asked, perplexed.

"It's not. I just thought of my own mother. The last

thing she gave me was a pair of itchy wool socks. Around the holidays, she orders weird things in bulk from catalogs and sends everyone she knows the identical weird thing for that year. She hates shopping, and she's not into sentiment, either."

Alejandro stroked her cheek, looking into her eyes and seeing far more than she wanted him to see. Kate slid off his lap and climbed into her own barstool again. The tables were all bar height, probably so patrons could have an uninhibited view of the dancers each night.

Two of the men swung down from the bar, and helped a girl up to dance with the sweaty chested man in the vest. She was one of the most naturally beautiful women Kate had ever seen, with a long, lithe body and gorgeous, wavy chestnut hair. Her costume was tiny but relatively tasteful, and the male dancer seemed to worship her with his eyes.

They danced as if they'd been created for one another, in perfect synergy and with quiet passion. Kate watched them with her heart in her throat, moved. Alejo smiled at her and took her hand.

"They are gorgeous together, are they not?"

She nodded. "How can they be so overtly sexy, but so poetic at the same time? It's phenomenal."

He squeezed her hand. "Yes. These two are world-class. Like you."

Kate was taken aback. "Like me? What are you talking about—I can't dance."

"I wasn't talking about dancing, Kate." His dark eyes were serious. "But I will teach you." He stood up and held out his hand.

"What? No!"

The two professionals on the bar ended their performance with an exotic pirouette, after which the man dipped the girl so far back that her head touched the surface of the bar, her body perfectly parallel to his extended leg.

Kate actually blinked away a tear, they were so magnificent together. The whole restaurant exploded with applause. And still Alejandro stood there patiently, his hand extended toward her. She shook her head.

"Come on, *mi amor*. I will teach you."

"I am not standing up in front of all these people and making a fool out of myself," she hissed.

"Why not?"

"Because!"

"Ah," he said. "Spinneys don't dance, either? You know, Spinneys, in my opinion, are repressed, intolerant and don't know how to have fun."

"Easy, sport," she said in a tight voice. But he spoke the truth. And how was she going to dance on a table by her thirtieth birthday if she couldn't even dance on a floor?

"Kate, do you know any of these people?"

She shook her head.

"Are you ever likely to see them again?"

She shrugged.

"Then why do you care if you make a fool out of yourself in front of them?"

"I just do."

"Spinneys are logical, too, I see."

Kate gritted her teeth.

"I won't let you make a fool out of yourself," he

promised. "Now come." He forcibly lifted her out of the chair and walked with her to the small dance floor in the back of the restaurant, setting her down just as she socked him in the stomach. "*Ooof*. Was that really necessary?"

He seized her by one hand and pulled her against his body, clamping his other hand firmly on her ass while she glared at him.

Then he began to dance a basic salsa, leading her along with him. She stumbled, stepped on his foot and tried to pluck his hand off her bottom, but he ignored her and just tightened his hold.

She found herself moving along with him despite her best efforts not to, in a sexy and deeply rhythmic sort of waltz. Her hips swayed with his, her feet tapped with his, her thighs brushed his.

She had an unfortunate tendency to try to lead, but Alejandro simply overwhelmed it and steered her backward every time she attempted to fight him.

He moved her in circles for a while, and then unexpectedly swung her out and under his arm, drawing her back to him for more close dancing. He pressed against her tightly, and she could feel his erection again, this time against her belly.

Before she knew it, Kate was actually laughing and having fun. She felt her inhibitions slip away along with her tendency to fight him and try to lead. Their movements began to become more fluid as she got used to him and anticipated his steps.

"*Perfecto, mi amor,*" he murmured into her ear. "You are very sexy once you just let go."

Nobody had ever called her *sexy* before. Kate knew

she was a lot of things: direct, forceful, smart. But she'd never thought of herself as sexy in the least. Not until now, with this miraculous man who made her *feel* sexy.

Alejandro swung her out again, and her hair flew out around her as he spun her right back into his arms, this time somehow managing to end with her back to him. He caught both of her hands and moved with her spoon-style, snugging his cock against her lower back, letting her know how much he wanted her. He spun her again as the song ended, pulling her to him for a deep, hard kiss.

Kate was doing it again: indulging in mad, passionate PDA with abandon. And she didn't care. Alejandro's mouth on hers was too wonderful, too full of erotic promises. He whispered into her ear what he was going to do to her later, and sexual electricity streaked through her body, igniting all of her fantasies.

If any of the Spinneys could see her now, they'd be deeply shocked—and that suited Kate just fine.

WHEN SHE RETURNED to her apartment the next morning, Wendell ambushed her with half a croissant in his hand. "Where have you been, young lady?"

*Is he for real?* She almost turned and walked back out the door. "Did you get a croissant for me, too?"

"No."

*It figures.*

"Kate, I asked you a question."

"And I obviously declined to answer it, Wendell."

"You've been rolling in the hay with that greaseball again. You look like a whore. You're acting like one, too. Don't you have any class at all?"

Kate gritted her teeth. Almost everyone had at least one undesirable relative, but this one took the cake. "Wendell, for starters, where I go is none of your business. Second, I don't want to know your opinion on anything at all. And third, *when the hell are you leaving?*"

He drew himself up, a hurt expression on his face. "You don't have to get so hostile, Katy."

"Yes, I obviously do! You've been camped out here for over a week now, tormenting me. Why?"

"Because I'm concerned about you."

"Ha! That's such a load. Tell me the real reason."

"I am," he insisted. "You're not behaving like yourself. Like a Spinney. We have a family name to uphold."

"No, Wendell, you're not here out of concern for me. You're here to keep your expense account in balance, since you probably bought something you shouldn't have with company funds."

Guilt flitted over Wendell's face.

"Gotcha! You know they won't look too closely at your fudged numbers if the totals are reasonably consistent. Well, if you're going to show up and use me as a hotel, then at least do me the favor of not verbally abusing me!"

"I don't—"

"Yes, you do. So stop it. And don't blackmail me, either. You can also quit complaining about my animals, and just *maybe,* when you go out for breakfast next time, bring me back something, too!"

He blinked and looked down at his half-gnawed

croissant. He extended it to her. "Do you want the rest? It's a little stale."

"I'm surprised you didn't call the authorities on the bakery."

"I thought about it," he admitted. "But my cell phone battery was low."

Kate put her hands to her temples. "So, again, when are you leaving?"

Wendell scuffed the toe of his shoe around on her kitchen floor. "I came to stay with you because I wanted to see you, too, Katy."

"Oh, spare me."

"It's true," he insisted. "You're the only decent one in the family. The only one who's ever even *borderline* nice to me."

Kate stared at him. Her stupid, gullible heart turned over at his words. It wasn't completely Wendell's fault that he was obnoxious. He'd been brought up by a grand total of twenty-three nannies, a revolving door of household help who'd only looked at him as an unpleasant way to earn a paycheck. Only a couple of them had been patient and dedicated enough to really try with the child, and when he'd lost them, too, he'd gotten even worse.

She blew out a breath. "Okay. You can stay until you're done with the due diligence on the proposed acquisition. But no more nasty comments, no more awful names for Alejandro and no kicking the dog I'm going to get."

"Ugh. You're bringing a dog home, now? We just got rid of the pig."

"Yes, Wendell, I am going to adopt a dog." *Preferably one with ringworm who will sleep on your bed.*

"Today, in fact, because I already miss Gracious and I need an animal to love. It's all part of the new Kate."

Wendell snorted his disgust with the new Kate and stuffed the rest of his stale croissant into his mouth. Then he disappeared into the guestroom to take a shower.

Kate looked at the white walls around her and thought of Alejandro's magical realist painting. She needed some art in here. And, okay, a couch. It would be nice to be able to study on a sofa, because trying to do so in bed always resulted in her falling asleep after the third page.

She frowned. She and Alejandro had been spending a lot of time together recently, but they sure hadn't been focused on the marketing plan…which was dangerous.

Pushing thoughts of him out of her mind, she grabbed her purse and headed for the door. Just as she got through it and turned to pull it closed behind her, Wendell popped out of the guestroom, his tubby body wrapped in one of her towels. "Thanks for letting me stay."

Great Scot! Wendell was being polite. Maybe he had potential to become human at some point?

"But you still owe me four thousand dollars," he announced.

Maybe not. "In your dreams, Wendell. Look, I'm sorry Gracious did that, but the suit can be dry-cleaned, the shirts and sheets can be washed and your shoes can be wiped off with leather cleaner."

He put his hands on his hips, assuming a mulish expression. He looked like a rogue Pillsbury Doughboy. "No. Everything must be replaced. I'm afraid I must insist."

"You can insist all you want, Wendell. You're not getting four thousand dollars out of me."

Wendell squinted at her and rocked back on his nude heels. "How would you like it if the board and the family were filled in on your activities with the greaseball?"

It was the last straw, and Kate finally lost her patience with him. "Trying to blackmail me again, Wendell? This time I won't stand for it. I'm reversing my decision—you *can't* stay.

"And regarding the pig, let me point out that *you* invited yourself here, you left your suitcase on the floor and you antagonized an innocent animal that has very few ways to express itself. So maybe you should take some responsibility for what happened. And by the way, if I were Gracious, I wouldn't have stopped with just pee!"

Wendell choked.

"So you go ahead and broadcast anything you want, you vicious little shit. But while you're doing it, you can get the hell out of my condo! We may come from the same family, and I might have a misguided soft spot for you, God knows why, but that does *not* give you the right to do or say anything you want to me and expect to continue a relationship. Your behavior has consequences. Got it? Now *get out*. If you're not gone by the time I get back, I will call the police. I mean it."

Kate slammed the door, vaguely surprised at herself. She was finally taking steps to put an end to the twisted, unhealthy relationship she had with certain family members. Spinneys might consider blood thicker than water, but Just Kate wasn't going to be a martyr to their cause.

# 17

"You, I will kill with my bare hands," Alejandro said to Peggy on the day of the client appreciation party. "And you, I will boil in oil," he said to Marly.

"Alejo, why so bloodthirsty?" she asked, blinking her lashes in feigned innocence. "You should be getting into rock 'n' roll mode! When is the DJ going to show up?"

"After I'm done murdering both of you," he said in menacing tones. "He'll put on a dirge while he helps me bury your bodies."

"And when will the luscious Kate arrive?"

"Never, if I can help it." He glared at them. "I cannot believe you two did this to me! Some friends you are. Bad enough that you had her sniffing around here for the marketing project, but now you're inviting her to parties? I'm not happy with you."

Marly poked him in the chest. "Alejo, you're going to have to tell her, and soon. You can't date a woman and not inform her of what you do for a living."

He shrugged uncomfortably.

"Unless you're planning to dump her for a bustier model? Trade her in for a bobblehead?"

"I am going to do no such thing. Kate is not the kind of woman any man in his right mind would dump."

Peggy and Marly exchanged a significant glance. Then they double-teamed him, the wenches. "So you're either in love or you're crazy, huh?"

"I'm not in love with her—it's too soon for that—but I'm not planning to let her go, either."

Marly waved a hand airily at him. "Oh, of *course* it's too soon to be in love with her. You've only been obsessed with her for months now."

Alejandro straightened his shoulders and stuck out his chin. "Obsessed? I don't think so. I have no need to be obsessed with anyone. I have many opportunities with women, as we all know."

"God," said Peggy. "If his head gets any bigger, he won't fit through the salon door."

"It's good for him to be obsessed with a woman," Marly said with a nod. "He's way too impressed with himself. Otherwise he'd just come clean and tell people what he did for a living, right? He wouldn't have such an ego that he'd hide it."

"I am not obsessed with Kate, and I am not in love! Why would I be in love with a woman that rude, that stubborn, that poorly dressed, with vile relatives who obviously clone themselves each generation? God forbid there should be a Wendell the fifth or the sixth...."

"We don't know why." Peggy shrugged. "But we like her because she challenges you. So would you go ahead and fall in love with her already?"

"No," Alejandro growled.

"Suit yourself. But if you're not going to do that, then you should go ahead and tell her that you give manicures and pedicures."

*"No,"* he growled, even louder. "It's embarrassing. It's not manly."

"Isn't he adorable?" Peg said to Marly.

"Cute as a bug," she agreed, smirking. "I have an idea. Let's out him on national television. Maybe on the *Jerry Springer Show.* What do you think?"

*"No!"* he thundered. "Go away and leave me alone, before I drown you both in the mud bath." He stomped into the back office in order to get away from his evil partners. Paying bills was preferable to being tortured by them.

But as he wrote out checks to the electric company and the city for water, guilt nagged at him. He should tell Kate what he really did. Whether he was in love with her or not, they did have a relationship at this point. And a relationship could not be based on lies or omissions.

*Beauty Boy! Beauty Boy!* The old demons chanted in his head. She would laugh at him. She would curl her lip. She would walk away. A woman like Kate Spinney would never lower herself to date a manicurist.

Still, there was no getting around it: he had to come clean. And soon. Even though she'd have nothing to do with him once he did.

A sharp noise alerted him to the fact that he'd just snapped the ballpoint pen he held in half. Blue ink spilled all over his right hand and soaked the checkbook, too. Alejandro cursed and stomped out of the office in search of paper towels. He couldn't wait until this stupid customer appreciation party started. He was just dying to have some damn fun.

He'd tell Kate tomorrow, he promised himself, as he blotted ink from his hands. Tomorrow, he'd get his guilty secret off his chest, and say goodbye to his fling with Kate. He looked down at the After Hours checkbook as he attempted to clean it up, and sighed. At least it was drowning in blue ink, not red.

Two HOURS LATER, the party was in full swing, with customers squealing over their goody bags and admiring each other's outfits. The wine and beer flowed, the music pulsed with sex-drenched lyrics and the sound of laughter overrode everything. The evening was a definite success and the customers felt appreciated.

As the host, Alejandro flashed his smile often and to potent effect, told jokes, kissed cheeks and fetched countless drinks. He even took to the dance floor with both Marly and Peggy without tripping them as he was tempted to do.

Soon he was dancing with eager female customers and fending off their less-than-subtle advances, as usual. He was just ending a song by dipping Heather Carlton almost to the ground, when Kate walked in and stopped his heart.

*Don't drop Heather.* The words flashed into his brain just as he almost did. He managed, mechanically, to right her and thank her for the dance, but then he stood gawping at the woman with whom he was emphatically not in love.

She looked like a goddess. There was no other word for it. Clad in the bronze leather skirt and the chocolate tank, her thin, rangy frame even further elongated by the high strappy heels she wore, she channeled Katharine Hepburn and Gisele Bundchen at the same time. Alejandro had no idea how she did it, but she managed to look simultaneously challenging, fragile and sexy.

He stood inelegantly riveted, unable to shake his gaze from her. She'd done her eyes, this time without smudges or streaks, in bronze and teal shadow and liner. Her lips were soft cinnamon and she'd lined them as well, so that they looked bee-stung. Just the sight of them made his groin tingle helplessly.

She'd done something miraculous with her hair and it framed her face, setting off her gorgeous cheekbones. And to top it all off, she'd dusted some kind of gold-bronze powder over her face and shoulders.

Alejandro did not shove his knuckles into his mouth. He did not step on his tongue. He did not drool onto the floor. But he did finally move like lightning to her side, because if any other man got near her, he was going to take him apart.

Kate smiled at him, and he felt it in his gut like a blow. "Do I look okay?" she asked.

He tried to swallow, but he couldn't. His mouth was too dry. All of his flowery compliments, delivered so skillfully in a slightly exaggerated accent that the women loved, crumbled into dust. He nodded.

She licked her lips and looked vaguely crushed. "It's the bronzing powder, isn't it. I made myself look like a clown—"

He put a stop to her self-criticism with his mouth and devoured the rest of her idiotic words. Clown? No.

Siren? Yes. Her lips tasted of cinnamon, too, and the peppermint toothpaste she'd used recently. He wanted her with an intensity that scared him.

When he finally pulled back for air, her eyes had gone smoky. She touched her mouth with a finger. "You messed up my Professional Pout, sport. D'you know how long it took me to get that lipliner on straight?"

He immediately engaged in another smear campaign. This time, he managed to drag the color all the way down to her chin, and give himself a good case of blue balls to boot.

She gasped and pushed him away. "Are you deliberately trying to make me look awful?"

He finally found his voice. "Yes. Where are your khaki pants and those gruesome loafers? You shouldn't be walking around like this."

"Like what?"

He gestured at her. "Like some kind of sex goddess, bent on the ruination of all mankind. Where is your blue oxford cloth shirt?"

She put her hands on her hips and glared at him.

*Dios mio, she's not wearing a bra....*

"I look like this because of *you,* sport! You couldn't stand my loafers or my clothes. So I humor you, and you're still not happy. What's your problem?"

He barely registered her words, because he was busy wondering if she had on any panties under that leather skirt of hers, and he was about to seriously embarrass himself in front of the entire party. He grabbed her wrist and towed her toward the back hallway.

"Excuse you! What the hell do you think you're—"

He ignored her and sped up, finally reaching the door of his small office after what seemed like an eternity. As he twisted the knob, he felt her small fist connect with his kidney. "Oof. Kate, *mi amor,* that is not my idea of foreplay!"

He shut the door, locked it and slid his hands up her leather skirt, rucking it up around her waist. She was still yammering about something, and he caught the word *caveman* in there somewhere, until he sealed her mouth with his own and stroked her between the legs. She trembled and sagged against him, which encouraged him to pick her up and set her on his desk while he ripped off the violet tanga she wore underneath the skirt.

He dropped into his office chair and pushed her back onto his papers. Then, with one strappy sandal on either arm of his chair, he bent his head to her and licked.

Kate gave a strangled cry and he did it again, savoring both her and her reaction. He had her completely in his power and could bestow pleasure or withhold it at will. He liked things that way. He was used to having power over women. He was *not* used to the effect that Kate had on him.

He'd never lost his ability to speak in his life. To punish her for that, he swirled his tongue around the area she was desperate for him to touch, careful to stay just out of reach of her clitoris.

Kate squirmed and whimpered and shifted her hips. He chuckled diabolically, then touched his tongue to her center for maybe half a second.

In love with her? Ridiculous. She was contrary and she drove him crazy and he wanted her back in those ugly, baggy clothes so that no other man would see the goddess underneath. His goddess. The one he was intent on torturing so that he didn't feel quite so screwy inside.

Alejandro took the whole of her into his mouth and she convulsed helplessly. He threw her ankles over his shoulders and honed in like a shark until he had her begging, her heels kicking against his back.

He was feeling fully in control again when she gasped something that he both did and did not want to hear. "Please, Alejo," she whispered. "Come inside. I need you inside."

How could he refuse the lady? He stood up, unbuckled his belt and freed himself from the tangle of cloth binding him. Then he sheathed himself in a condom and drove into her, her soft cries urging him on.

His eyes damn near rolled back into his head, she felt so good. Alejandro lost himself in her tight heat and to his shame, lasted about five strokes. As she orgasmed around him, seizing his cock with her inner muscles, she turned him on so much that he completely lost control.

He stared down at her beautiful face in a mixture of ecstasy and gloom: so much for wresting back sexual control from this woman. She had him tied around her little finger. It was a damn good thing he wasn't in love with her, that was for sure.

# 18

KATE COULDN'T BELIEVE that she'd just had sex with Alejandro on someone's desk in someone's office during a party! Spinneys didn't boink on desks, and they certainly didn't sneak away for quickies during social gatherings. But…the new Kate apparently did.

She fixed her hair and tried to reapply her makeup in the ladies' room, but her hands shook from postorgasmic adrenaline.

The mirror told her that she still had her father's features and her mother's hair, but nobody in her family wore makeup like this, clothes like this or spike heels. Who was she, exactly, if not a Spinney of Spinney Industries? She was…Just Kate. The world felt wide open to her, ready for exploration. Just Kate could do anything—except, apparently, apply lipliner.

She'd slipped with the pencil again. Kate swore, trying to rub off the crooked line. Were there really women who took an hour to apply their makeup each day? She couldn't fathom it.

Kate gave makeup five minutes or less. If she couldn't get it on during that time, then it wasn't worth wearing. There were too many other things to do.

Finally she got the line straight and the matching lipstick applied inside, just like a coloring book. She did a little victory dance and put the stupid cosmetics back in the useless little evening bag Alejandro had forced her to buy. She frowned. Okay, so he'd attacked her like some kind of sex-starved animal, but he'd never actually said she looked nice. She wanted to hear the words.

Kate opened the door of the ladies' room and spied him immediately, since some vixen in a backless red dress had draped herself upon his chest like a blanket. *Ooh,* what she wouldn't give right now for a pair of nail scissors.

Shocked at her own cattiness, she marched out and went straight to the bar, where she got a glass of red wine. Then she managed to drift accidentally back to where Alejo and Miss Scarlet stood, and caught the tail end of their conversation.

"I can't wait," purred the woman.

He smiled down at her and patted her arm, which was, in Kate's opinion, quite unnecessary since her bosom was almost shoved up his nose.

*Wait for what?*

"I love the way your hands feel on my skin, Señor Manos."

Kate stood in shock, holding a large swallow of wine in her mouth, afraid she might choke on it. Then she told herself to calm down. Alejandro *had* just touched the woman's arm. Kate let the wine trickle down her throat.

But why was she calling him Señor Manos? What did that mean again? Mr. Hands?

*It's a product that we use in the course of a manicure or pedicure. Imported from Peru.* That's what Alejandro had told her when she'd visited the salon to make notes for the marketing class.

Wait a minute. Had he said *we?* Yes, he most certainly had. *We.* Which implied that Alejandro had more of an interest in After Hours than just doing the books. She wondered if Peggy and Marly had borrowed money from him, if he had a stake in the spa. But that still didn't explain why Miss Scarlett was calling him Señor Manos.

Imported from Peru…Alejandro was half Peruvian. Kate pursed her lips. Of course: he supplied them exclusively with the lotion or whatever it was. And this woman probably knew that and teased him by calling him the name of the product.

Kate fought with her possessive instincts, which had her wanting to chase the woman away from him. *Grow up.* She wandered away from the two and saw Marly a few feet away, one of the only other people she knew at the party. She went over to say hi.

"Kate, you look gorgeous," Marly told her, seeming genuinely glad that she had come. "Has Alejandro seen you yet?"

*Um, yeah, you could say that. Up close and personal.* "We've said hello. He's talking with one of your customers."

"I can't believe he left your side after getting a load of you in that skirt. But he does have client schmoozing to do…" She broke off, biting her lip.

"Marly, he's more than just your accountant, isn't he? Does he have a stake in the business? Or does he just supply that Señor Manos product you guys were talking about?"

Marly opened and shut her mouth. "Right," she said in bright tones. "And boy, has that taken off."

"Is there a special ingredient?" Kate asked. "Because I'm thinking that maybe that could be part of your new marketing approach—hand out free samples of this stuff to prospective clients."

Marly blinked. "What a...what a great idea! You should talk to Alejandro about that. Excuse me, I see a customer that I need to speak to." And she vanished, unable to get away fast enough, despite her initial enthusiasm for seeing Kate.

Mystified, Kate stared after her. Was there a problem with the patent on the Señor Manos lotion, or something? Were they afraid that a competitor might get hold of it and break down the components; steal the recipe?

Really, that was the only explanation. Kate took another sip of her wine and felt her competitive instincts surface. Was Señor Manos a new miracle cream? A cream that, for example, Spinney Industries could make real money off of?

She had yet more wine as she thought about the circumstances surrounding her getting to know Alejandro. He'd definitely known who she was, with his teasing comment about her *no-account* family. Had he, perhaps, initiated a relationship with her so that he could eventually get funding for the marketing and distribution of his own product?

She felt a little sick inside at the thought. Her father's words to her when she was ten echoed through her mind. *Don't be naive. You've been born a very wealthy little girl. People—and men in particular—will try to use you for your money.*

Kate gulped the rest of her wine and felt even sicker. Had she just been intimate with a man who really wanted nothing more than a business relationship with her? Had she allowed herself to be manipulated and used?

"Oh, Kate! There you are. How nice to see you," Peggy exclaimed. "You look absolutely beautiful."

"Thanks."

"Have you signed up for your complimentary manicure?"

Kate looked down at her bare, somewhat ragged nails. "Nope."

"Well, I told you we'd book you one, doll. And Marly will do your hair, if you want—not that it doesn't look great already."

Kate gave her a wobbly smile.

"You want some more wine? I'll get it for you."

Though she felt like drinking about two quarts of the stuff to drown her suspicions, Kate shook her head. "No, thanks."

"Okay. You look stressed, hon. Go sign up for any beauty treatment you want. Shirlie, our receptionist, will help you."

"Thanks." And Peggy was gone, swallowed by the chic, shimmering, gyrating crowd. Kate looked over at where Alejandro had been standing with Miss Scarlett, only to find that she'd been replaced by an equally flirtatious woman in a gold halter top and chandelier earrings. He threw back his head and laughed at something she said.

Kate restrained a snarl and marched over to the reception desk, only to find Shirlie gone.

She'd have her free manicure, and maybe a facial and a massage while she was at it. The appointment book was right there, even if Shirlie wasn't. Kate slipped behind the desk and flipped a couple of pages until she found a date that had open back-to-back slots. She'd do the facial first, then the massage and last of all the manicure.

She didn't particularly care who did the procedures, and the technicians seemed to be listed by initials only, so she plugged herself in: B.T. for the facial, P.U. for the massage and S.M. for the manicure. P.U. was probably Peggy, but she didn't know who the other two were.

She left the appointment book on the desk and searched the crowd again for Alejandro. He'd switched out Gold Halter Top for Miss Ice-Blue Camisole now, but he caught her eye from across the room and winked at Kate.

She was tempted to confront him here and now. After all, she wasn't shy about such things. But as a good WASP, she had a horror of dramatic public scenes. Calmly correcting a professor was one thing. But she had an awful feeling that if she started with this topic right now, her emotions would get the better of her and she'd scream like a fishwife.

Kate kept her face neutral and swallowed her feelings. She yawned and jerked her head toward the door, indicating that she was tired and leaving.

He made his way to her side in an instant. "Kate, *mi amor,* you don't wish to come home with me?"

"I'm not feeling very well," she lied. "I'm just going to drive back to my condo and go to bed."

"It is your head? Your stomach?" His eyes reflected concern.

*It's my pragmatism, sport. It's your secret product.* "Oh, I just feel a little nauseous."

"I will drive you."

"No. You're having fun, and it's early. Really, I'll be fine."

He insisted on walking her to her car, no matter what she said, and he kissed her good night. She could hardly bear to look at him. Were her suspicions grounded?

"Get some sleep, *mi corazon.* I will call you *manana.*" He closed her door and waited until she'd started the car. He looked worried.

*And so you should be,* Kate thought, as she put her old Mercedes into reverse and drove into the night.

# *19*

KATE LOOKED AT her new, still nameless dog, who wouldn't stop licking her adoringly on the arm as she drove from the animal shelter to her condo. No Name was a somewhat bizarre-looking mix of boxer and collie, with maybe a little moose thrown in. Her personality made up for her looks, though. She slurped Kate's arm again.

"You don't have to say thank you, sweetheart. I need you, too. I'm really sorry about the spaying thing, but they wouldn't let you come home with me if we didn't do that. It's why I couldn't take you the other day."

The dog kept licking.

"You forgive me? Tell you what, to make it up to you, I have a T-bone for your dinner. I figure that's kind of like me eating half a pan of brownies for dinner—we can't do it every day, but it helps make us feel better in the short run. So what's your name, huh? Snowball is just not going to work for me. First of all, you've got lots of brown with the white. And it's hot here. And Mudball doesn't seem like a very nice name. So work with me, here. What do you want to be called?"

The dog cocked her head, seeming to understand.

"I met a pig named Gracious," Kate told her. "She even stayed with me for a few days."

Her new pet wagged her tail.

"Yeah, you'd like her. Maybe I'll introduce you sometime…." She thought darkly of Alejandro, since it was his neighbor who owned Gracious. "But maybe not." She still had to have a little talk with him, but she honestly didn't know how to bring up the subject. Maybe she was wrong, anyway. She should probably just wait to see if he actually did ask her to invest in Señor Manos.

What a dumb name for a lotion. The name definitely had to be changed to something with more panache. And what was the current packaging like? Come to think of it, she'd never seen a single jar or bottle of the stuff at After Hours.

Which was just fine by her, she reminded herself sternly, because she was not going to invest in it. She turned the car into the parking lot of her building, keeping a sharp eye out for old Mr. Landry. Thank God he wasn't out there.

She clipped a leash to No Name's collar and urged her out of the car. She immediately began sniffing around her new pad, gathering all kinds of clues about her new environment.

"See, you're good at that," Kate told her. "Maybe you can track down a couch for me?" They went inside and she stopped at the concierge desk. "Hi, Kevin."

"Hello, Ms. Spinney. How are you today?"

"Fine, thanks. Any messages? Packages?"

He shook his head and then stopped, a peculiar expression on his face. "There was another complaint lodged against you the other day, though."

"You're kidding. For what?"

"Same thing. A caller accused you of having a pig in your unit."

Kate narrowed her eyes. Wendell had struck again. She jiggled the leash. "Kevin. Does this look like a pig to you?"

"No, ma'am, it doesn't."

"Do you want to search my condo for a pig?"

"I don't think that'll be necessary."

"If you get the urge, just knock, okay? I'll open the door after I get the rubber pig mask off my dog, here."

Kevin laughed. "Yes, ma'am."

A few minutes later in her condo, Kate looked at No Name thoughtfully while she heated the broiler for her T-bone. "You've got to help me out, here, sweetie. You need a name, and I need some good revenge."

The dog eyed her sympathetically and then walked to the kitchen counter, where the steak sat ready. She sniffed, eager to make its acquaintance.

"We have to cook it. Haven't you ever heard of E. coli or mad cow disease? The last thing I need here is a mad dog who moos."

No Name sat down, never taking her eye off the steak.

"So. You want salt?" Kate got it out of a cupboard and sprinkled some on the T-bone. Then she put the salt back and located a box of brownie mix. "Me, I always add some extra cocoa powder to my chocolate batter. They never make it fudgy enough."

No Name scratched her ear.

"There's only one company who makes their brownies with enough chocolate, and that's Ghirardelli. If you add cocoa powder to their mix, you're likely to die of chocolate poisoning."

Kate stopped. Was she really having a conversation with a dog?

"But you can't eat any chocolate at all, No Name. It's bad for dogs." Kate checked the broiler. It was blazing hot, so she shoved the steak under it. "Medium-rare okay with you?"

The dog collapsed in a puddle of paws, fur and drool. She rolled onto her back, exposing a shaved pink expanse of flesh with stitches poking out.

"I thought so." While the steak broiled, Kate cracked an egg into a bowl, added oil and water and then shook the brownie mix in on top. She stirred the batter, then flipped the steak.

She was in the process of pouring the batter into a pan when her phone rang. She sighed. What fresh hell would be on the other end of the line?

It was Kevin from downstairs. "There's a gentleman here to see you, Miss Spinney. A Mr. Torres?"

Oh, hell. Part of her wanted to confront him. Part of her wanted to stick her head in the sand and pretend her suspicions didn't exist. And part of her wanted to just bide her time and see if she was right.

"Miss Spinney?"

Kate looked down at the dog hairs covering her jeans, remembered that she hadn't even showered this morning and then decided she didn't care. "Send him up, Kevin. Thanks."

Her dog barked at Alejandro when she opened the door. She stood close to Kate and watched him warily, the fur on her neck at attention. "Shh. It's okay," Kate told her. "He's a friend." *I think.*

"Kate? You have a dog?" He leaned forward to kiss her. She let him.

"The emptiness of this place was getting to me. This is No Name."

"And here I was going to get you a pig." He bent down and extended his hand so the dog could sniff it, and then scratched her behind the ears. His stomach growled. "Something smells good. I didn't think you cooked."

"I don't. Well, aside from scrambled eggs and toast, steak and brownies are the only things in my culinary repertoire."

"Steak?" He brightened.

"Don't get your hopes up, sport. It's for No Name. I promised it to her because of the spay operation."

His handsome jaw dropped. "You're broiling a steak for a dog? I can think of much better uses for it," he said, rubbing his stomach.

"You can have a brownie."

"You choose a dog over your boyfriend?"

She'd been walking back to the kitchen, but she stopped in her tracks. Boyfriend? Was that what Alejandro was? She continued on her way without answering and pulled the steak out from under the broiler, setting it on the cooktop to cool.

Alejandro followed her and gazed at it, then back at her, not as amused as he pretended to be. She sighed.

•

"I promised her," she said defensively. No Name, who had followed them into the kitchen, wagged her tail.

"Besides, I don't cook for men. I don't do their laundry or iron for them, either. I'm a feminist."

"What if you were married to the man? And he cooked and did the laundry sometimes, too?"

She frowned. "Oh. Well, I suppose that would be different." She followed his eyes to the steak again, and waffled. He had brought dinner one of the nights that Wendell had been here. She owed him. But she was also suspicious of his motives and rather upset.

Kate speared the steak and put it on a plate, Alejo's eyes following the meat just as avidly as the dog's. Ignoring him, she heartlessly began to cut it up into bite-size pieces. "Look, I'm not having any of this, either. It's not like I'm discriminating against you, sport."

He narrowed his eyes at her and continued to watch her decimate the meat. His stomach growled again. "Why are you angry with me, Kate?" he asked quietly.

"I'm not angry with you," she said, and set the plate down for No Name, who sprang at it with ill-disguised canine glee. Alejandro made a choking noise.

In one motion, the dog's tongue licked over every morsel on the plate, and Alejandro's expression of longing faded, to be replaced by one of disgust.

"You're calling me sport," he said. "You only do that when you're irritated."

Damn. He had picked that up about her, hadn't he? Kate flicked her gaze to him briefly before watching her new dog push the plate across the kitchen floor, devouring every scrap of meat.

She should come clean with him about her suspicions. But the words refused to form in her head, much less come out of her mouth. For the first time in her life, she didn't want to know the truth.

He stood there, so big and handsome and rippling with muscle, and she desperately wanted to believe that he desired her for her character, her looks, her sense of humor—anything except for her name or her money. Tears threatened to form in back of her eyes, and she willed them fiercely away.

"Why are you angry?" he asked again. "Is it the women who were flirting with me at the party?"

"Yeah," she said shortly. "The one in the red dress was stuck to you like Velcro." She was happy to have an excuse to be annoyed with him—any reason besides the real one.

"I'm sorry about that," he said, reddening. "I—er— she's a regular customer. I can't be rude to her—she brings a lot of business to the salon."

Kate lifted a sardonic brow. "And the woman in the gold halter top and chandelier earrings? She practically humped your leg."

"Also a customer." The red climbed down his cheeks and spread to his neck.

"Great. And the one in blue?"

He shrugged helplessly, holding his palms up and clearly asking for her understanding. "I cannot offend them. It would be bad for business, and Peg and Marly are my friends."

"You have a stake in the business, don't you. You're not just an accountant for them." She said it as a statement, not as a question.

He nodded slowly. "Yes, I do. That is true. I should have mentioned it to you earlier." He looked deeply uncomfortable, and she swallowed. They were getting onto dangerous ground here. Was she ready to do this? How could she have let him shake her up emotionally? Unbalance her to this degree?

*Just confront him, Kate. Do it. You had no problem with Professor Kurtz.*

But she hadn't slept with Kurtz. She hadn't let Kurtz make all kinds of changes in her life and tie her into knots like a pretzel. She didn't give a rat's ass about Kurtz…whereas Alejandro was different. She shied away from identifying her feelings for Alejandro. They were too jumbled. All she knew was that she was vulnerable to him.

"Kate, there's…something I have to tell you."

Sudden panic rose in her, almost choking her. She shut her eyes. *No! No! I don't want to hear this. You can't make me.*

Her father's lockjawed tones echoed in her head. *Men who wear gold chains are either pimps or weasels….*

"Kate," he said. "This is something embarrassing. Something I'm not proud of—"

*Embarrassing?* That was one way to put it! Nice of him to be concerned for his own ego, and not her feelings. It was merely *embarrassing* to him that he'd sought her out with capitalism in mind? Well, hell. The irony didn't escape her. They *were* in business school.

She couldn't take it. "Stop," she said abruptly. "Just shut up. I don't want to hear it."

He drew his eyebrows together. "But—"

"I think you should go now." She was getting good at kicking guys out of her condo.

His mouth hung open. "What? Why? Kate, *mi amor*—"

She marched to the door and held it open. "Out." He was worse than Wendell. At least her cousin was upfront about his obnoxiousness.

He stared at her, his expression growing thunderous. "What is the matter with you? I told you that those women—that I do not encourage them, and I certainly don't sleep with them."

*"Out!"* she shouted. No Name growled at him, clearly willing to chew off his leg for a woman who fed her T-bones.

He threw up his hands and stalked to the door. "Fine. But I don't understand why you are behaving like a *bruja*. If and when you get over it, you call me."

Kate wasn't sure, but she thought *bruja* meant *witch*. That exacerbated her anger. "Yeah, next time I go skiing in hell, sport."

She slammed the door on him and went to get her rather singed brownies out of the oven. After eating the entire pan, maybe she'd go buy herself a couch and a matching broomstick.

# 20

ALEJANDRO DROVE HOME fuming. Women! Here he was trying to be honest with Kate, tell her his darkest and most humiliating secret, and she wouldn't even let him. Wouldn't listen to a word he had to say, all because he had spoken politely to a few customers at the party.

But worse! *Far worse,* she had chosen to give a mouthwatering T-bone to a *dog* over him. That really showed him where he stood with her, how far down he was on her list of priorities. He still couldn't quite believe it, and she'd done it with a smug expression on her face, too. He and his stomach growled simultaneously at the insult, and he wrenched the wheel of the Porsche to pull into a fast-food burger place.

Slightly mollified by the taste of greasy fries on the way back to After Hours, he took out the rest of his temper on the unfortunate drivers around him, zipping and weaving in and out of traffic like a drunken frat boy. Horns honked at him and fists waved, a trucker insulted his heritage and an improbably blond old lady shot him the finger.

It wasn't until he was on his way to work a couple of days later that he felt better. It wasn't his fault that women flirted with him, for God's sake! And hadn't he shown Kate how much he'd wanted her? He wasn't in the habit of nailing women on his desk in the middle of social events.

What did she want from him? Did she require that he put a ring through his nose and let her lead him through the party afterward? Or perhaps brand himself on the forehead with a large K.S., so that other women would know he was hers? Oh, right—he should have *proposed* as soon as they were dressed again.

Alejo tried to emit a scornful snort, but found that it stuck in his nose and rattled around instead, sending an extremely disturbing message to his brain. Oh, no, no, no. He sent it right back, unopened.

He wrenched open the door to After Hours and Shirlie sang, *"Buenos dias,* Alejandro!" aiming her cute little smile in his direction. It faded immediately. "God, what is wrong with you? You look like you just swallowed a hornet!"

He stared at her a bit wildly. "I'm fine. I'll be in the back. I have an appointment in half an hour, but I don't know her name. It's illegible." And he brushed past her, moving on autopilot past everyone, from the other nail techs to Marly and Nicky—from whom he averted his eyes since the hairdresser was wearing a purple suede vest over a teal silk shirt. What was he, Merlin's mad assistant?

Alejandro strode to the little backroom where his pedicure station sat, shut the door and slumped into the big chair his clients used. *No,* he thought. *I cannot possibly be entertaining thoughts of spending my life with a woman who feeds steak to a dog over me. It's just not right.*

*And Mama told me one day I'd find a sweet, darling girl who'd worship me. Ha!*

Gloomily, he disinfected the pedicure basin and wiped down all of his tools with Barbasol before setting them down on a clean towel. He put on some soothing music. He ruminated for a while on skinny, flat-chested, troublesome, jealous women with impossible hair and more affection for animals than men. They were so not worth his time.

Finally he glanced at his watch and got up to go and get a double espresso from Benito's. "Shirlie," he told the receptionist, "if my client arrives early, just show her to the backroom. I won't be long."

He meandered over to get his coffee and stayed for a few minutes chatting with Benny. He nodded at Shirlie as he came in the door. She was on the phone, but looked up to jerk a thumb toward the back and nod. Was that a smirk she was hiding? Alejandro looked down at his shirt to see if he'd spilled any of the espresso on it, but it was clean.

As he passed Marly, she bent her head to get a clip out of her drawer, her braid hanging in her face. He grabbed a fresh white hand towel and threw it over his shoulder, then scooped up a set of foam toe separators and a fresh buffer. He sighed and went to the door of the back room. Time to assume the position. His balls sagged.

He took a sip of the espresso for fortification and turned the knob. He spit it all over the floor and dropped everything else when he saw the occupant of the chair.

"K-Kate?" *Mierda, mierda, mierda!* His goose was cooked.

*"Alejandro?"* She sat with her pants rolled up to the knees, her feet in the basin of warm, sudsy water. Her hair looked even more in disarray than usual, her green eyes seemed sleepy and the skin of her arms glowed faintly with oil in the low lighting. She looked, in fact, like she'd just rolled out of bed after a long, slow afternoon of making love. In spite of the awfulness of this situation, his balls contracted.

She looked at the foam toe separators and the buffer he'd dropped, her expression changing from sleepy to incredulous.

He rubbed furiously at some coffee on his shirt with the white hand towel, fire suffusing his face and neck. *Beauty Boy! Beauty Boy! Beauty Boy!* "I—I was just bringing in these things for your, um, nail tech." He winced. *Maricon! Chivo! Rosquete!*

Her eyes narrowed on him, and she lay her head back in the chair, inspecting him. "Is that right."

"Yes. She'll be right in." Peggy had better be here, he didn't care if she had a client or not. He'd massage her client and she could give Kate a goddamned pedicure. Had he really been about to tell Katherine Spinney what he did when he wasn't in class? Her nose was *already* up in the air.

"Then why," Kate asked, "is your face redder than a boiled Maine lobster?"

"Eh? Oh—I was just moving some boxes around in the office. Heavy boxes."

She folded her arms and stared at him like he was a particularly large and unappetizing water bug. "You give pedicures here."

He waved a hand at her. "Don't be ridiculous. Do I look like the kind of man who gives pedicures?" He laughed, too loudly.

"I don't know. What kind of man, in particular, gives pedicures?"

Alejandro made a rude noise. "You know what kind. Men who are not men."

"Ah. I see. You're referring to gays?"

He gave a half shrug, wondering why he felt as if he were walking the plank.

"And…what exactly do men who are not men look like?"

He refused to meet her gaze. "Well, you know."

"No, I don't know."

"Like…Nicky, our hairdresser."

"Really. All of them? That's funny, Alejandro, because I have a brother who's gay, and he can bench-press three-hundred-and-fifty pounds. He never wears pink, he couldn't flap his hand if his life depended on it and he was captain of his college lacrosse team." Her tone was just shy of biting.

He swallowed and fiddled with the gold chain around his neck. He set down his espresso and examined a nick in the wallboard.

"So, do you want to tell me the truth?"

"Damn, they did a terrible job of floating and taping this wall."

"Alejandro!"

He looked up, and her eyes blazed at him, green and hostile. Definitely hostile.

"How's T-bone?" he asked. "Did she enjoy her lunch?"

"T-bone," she repeated, her anger arrested momentarily. "That's *perfect.*" Then she glared at him again. "She's fine. Now come clean with me, Alejo." She kicked water at him from the pedicure basin.

He cracked his neck. "I am part owner of After Hours. I also bring in a nice income for the spa by giving—" he gulped "—manicures and pedicures. All day. Sometimes until midnight." He stole a look at her, only to find that she resembled granite.

"And why the hell didn't you tell me this weeks ago?"

He sighed. "Because you're a Spinney. Women from families like yours don't…date manicurists. I was embarrassed. I thought you'd look down on me."

She was silent for too long. Then she pulled her feet out of the pedicure basin and snatched the towel he'd left folded on the rim. She dried her legs and feet, unrolled her pants and slid out of the chair. "You sure don't think much of me, do you, Alejandro?"

"That's not true—"

"You think I'm a goddamned snob!"

"No, I don't. I just wanted to have a chance with you, that's all."

She whirled on him, eyes now like lasers. "Why?"

"I've told you why."

"Is there anything else you'd like to add to that?"

"No. I thought you were beautiful and smart and—"

"Connected? Rich? Able to market and distribute your exclusive product, perhaps?"

"What?" He goggled at her. Then, when her meaning

sank in, anger flashed through him. "I could care less about your family name or your money! If anything, that made me *avoid* asking you out. But I wanted you—"

"Yeah," she said, cynicism dripping from her voice. "Sure you did. It had nothing to do with your freakin' hand cream."

He stared at her again. "What are you talking about?"

"Lotion. Whatever it is. That Señor Manos stuff you import from Peru. You know exactly what I'm talking about."

Incredulous, he began to laugh, even though he was far too furious to laugh. "You think that I came on to you for the sake of Señor Manos?"

She just looked at him, disgust radiating from every pore.

"Well, then, *señorita,* you don't have a very high opinion of me, either, now do you?"

"No," she said baldly. "I don't."

He laughed until he had tears streaming down his cheeks and probably looked like a homicidal madman. He wondered vaguely why she still stood there, why she hadn't slammed out of the place, until he realized that he was leaning against the door.

"So let me get this straight," he gasped. "You believe that I took you to bed in order to manipulate you into getting Spinney Industries to back my product."

"I know it, sport. And that's why you were so secretive about having a stake in After Hours, isn't it? I'm not stupid."

"Eh, well. You've got it all figured out, don't you,

Harvard? My bluff has been called. You're right. But at least you got some hot sex out of it."

She drew back her hand and slapped him, hard.

He looked down at her with disdain, ignoring the burn of it. Her freckles stood out starkly against her pale skin, there were two white dents at her flared nostrils, and she seemed unable to catch her breath.

"It's tempting to smack you right back. I'm sure you can take what you dish out, since you're a *feminist*. But I wasn't brought up nearly as badly as you. And I don't hit women."

She sucked in her breath in a hiss.

"Besides, I'd rather leave you with something to think about, not something to nurse. There's one tiny flaw in your logic, Harvard."

"Oh?"

He nodded. "Yes. There *is* no product. *I'm* Señor Manos."

He left her standing with her mouth agape and walked straight out of the salon.

# 21

"*HE'S* SEÑOR MANOS?" Kate grabbed Marly by the shoulder and spun her around. "How can he be Señor Manos, when he told me himself it was a product imported from Peru? He lied to me! I may have slapped him, but he lied to me!"

"Shh," said Marly, her eye on a lovely blonde sitting at one of the manicure tables. The blonde's eyes had widened and she stared avidly after Alejandro's retreating form. Then she dug into her wickedly expensive handbag, pulled out a cell phone and began speaking rapidly to someone in Spanish.

Marly groaned. She asked her client to excuse her for a moment and took Kate into the back office, shutting the door behind them.

Kate stared at the desk where she and Alejo had made love just a couple of short nights ago. She closed her eyes.

Marly sighed. "Damn it, I wish you hadn't said that out there. That little blonde is the girlfriend of one of Alejandro's soccer buddies. And she's wasting no time in telling her man that Alejo is Señor Manos. He's been afraid of this happening all year."

"He told me it was a *product*," Kate repeated.

"Listen, hon, he'd have told you chicken crap was good in a sandwich if he thought it would throw you off track about him giving manicures. It would be bad enough for a big strapping Anglo kid to admit. But Alejo is Peruvian. Ever heard of the term *machismo?* Take average pigheaded male pride and multiply it times ten, or maybe twenty. That will give you some idea of how acceptable it is in his culture for a straight man to give manicures."

"Look, I can understand that, but—"

"No, I don't think you can. To have this information come out to you or any of his buddies—" Marly shook her head. "It's like him tearing off his pants in public and displaying, er, equipment an inch long and half an inch in diameter."

Kate choked, knowing very much different.

"It's like him shouting to the world that he's not a real man."

"That is ridiculous," Kate said.

Marly shrugged. "We've been warning him for months now that it would come out sooner or later, but that's how he's felt about it. He wanted to hide it as long as possible—especially from you."

Kate clenched her fists. "I could kill him."

Marly lifted an eyebrow. "Sounds like you made a start, if you're slapping him around. But I would have figured you as more of a closed-fist-into-the-stomach type of girl."

"I am," Kate growled. "But thanks to Miami, I'm getting all too girlie."

"Anyway—why did you slap him?"

"Because I think—I thought—he was dating me for what the Spinney name could do for his goddamned stupid lotion that doesn't exist!"

"Ouch."

"And he let me think it was true until he got the last word." Kate threw up her hands.

Marly's lips twitched. "Of course. Men always have to have the last word."

"And now I'm going to have to apologize, except I'm too freakin' *furious* to apologize, and he freakin' needs to freakin' apologize to me first, for lying to me!"

"Uh-*huh*," said Marly, looking skeptical about this possibility.

"And I *hate* freakin' apologizing! Spinneys don't freakin' apologize!"

"Neither do pissed off, pigheaded, Peruvian males."

"I thought he was only half-Peruvian," Kate fumed.

"Irrelevant. He's *all* pigheaded male."

"Well, I never want to see him again!"

Marly nodded. "Except to kill him. I'll pass along the message."

"Do that, will you?"

"On one condition—that you believe me when I tell you that Alejandro has talked about you since the very first week of your MBA program, and he never once mentioned your name or your money."

"Why should I believe you? You're his friend and business partner."

Marly elevated her chin and shot her a steely glance. "Believe whatever you want, Kate. But to suggest that

Peggy and I are in on some vast conspiracy to snow you, use you and fleece you of your money is to suggest that you have a paranoia bigger than the state of Florida— and an ego to match. It's just possible that we actually *liked* you."

Kate's mouth dropped open for the third time that day. Marly held her head high and sailed to the door. She opened it and left the room without a backward glance.

ALEJANDRO DID NOT return to work that day. He was too furious, and Kate's palm print was still clearly outlined on his face a half hour after their confrontation.

How could she have thought he'd sought her out for her family connections and money? The unfairness of it stung him. After what they'd shared together, in bed and out, she still thought he was a lowlife and an opportunist. A user.

*Well, good Christ, Alejo, look at her cousin. If all her relatives are that bad, no wonder she thinks everyone's got an agenda.*

But he ignored the voice inside him that tried to analyze and explain—if not justify—her behavior. She should have known he was different. He wouldn't take a red cent of her damned money—he planned to make his own. And as for the Spinneys and their family connections—he snorted. They could all go get stuffed.

He put his hand to the cheek Kate had slapped and burned with anger. Then the insidious voice came again. *Can you really blame her, given what she thought and what you said?*

Yes! Hell yes, he could damn well blame her. Because if she hadn't thought it of him in the first place, they wouldn't have been in such an argument.

*Put yourself in her position, man. She's probably had people sucking up to her for her money for years. She's probably gotten a little cynical. A little wary of smooth talkers.*

But Alejandro didn't feel like thinking about her perspective on things. She was a *bruja*.

*What about her uncertainty about sex and her doubts about her physical appeal? What had she said...I've been warned about smooth-talking Latin men like you.*

Had she been warned from birth that men would lie to her to get to her money?

Again, he told himself that he didn't care. He never wanted to see her again, and he wouldn't.

Then he remembered the stinking marketing project. The one he'd pressed her so hard about. The one they now had to do together. *Mierda!*

To distract himself, Alejandro went over to Tia Carlotta's and worked on various projects that needed to be done, while she popped out intermittently to try to feed him something. He refused all offers of anything except water.

"What," she asked him, hands on her ample hips. "You diet? Your mother was always on diet, God rest her soul."

"I'm not on a diet, Tia. I'm just not hungry. Thank you, though." He wiped the sweat from his eyes and continued to work on trimming the trees back from her roof.

"You are angry for something?"

"No, no. I'm fine."

She sighed. "Won't talk about nothing, just like your mother. Held it all inside, God rest her soul."

As usual, he could almost hear Mama's soul sawing logs with all the resting, but he chased away the irreverent thought. "Tia, it's hot out here. You should go inside and get out of the sun."

She continued to buzz around him until the arrival of the arborist he'd hired to remove the tree they'd argued about. The arborist was a big, strapping, once-blond gringo with a tanned, leathery face. Alejo judged him to be about Tia Carlotta's age. More importantly, it only took her five minutes to get him to admit he was hungry. Alejandro heaved a sigh of relief.

When he was finished, he went inside to find that the tree man had devoured half of her fresh-made *cau-cau* with great appreciation. Alejo raised an eyebrow and finally accepted a slice of flan and an *Inca Cola*. Then he kissed Tia's cheek, subtly chased the guy back out into the yard and went home to change for soccer practice.

HE KNEW SOMETHING was wrong as soon as he got out of the car and the guys turned as one to look at him, sneers etched on their faces. He froze. Hadn't this day been crappy enough? Now he had to deal with *this?* What he felt like doing was getting back into his car and driving north to Georgia.

Instead, he took a deep breath, slammed the Porsche's door and strode onto the field, ignoring the bleating goat sounds a couple of his teammates were making.

"Eh, *maricon*," a man named Franco called. "Let's see your nails." He hooted with laughter. "Did you have the French manicure today?"

*Beauty Boy! Beauty Boy!* Alejo dropped his soccer ball on the ground and passed it somewhat viciously to the jerk. "No, *pendejo*, I did a nice shade of ruby red on my *customer*. After she had an orgasm in her chair just from me touching her." He grinned maliciously, and Franco kicked the ball back at him as if it were infected.

Alejandro spun it on his toe and then kept it in the air with his knees and some good footwork. "Franco, did you have fun at the insurance company today? I'll bet you don't get to touch beautiful women's legs all day, like me." That shut Franco up, since he wasn't that quick on his feet, but there were still fifteen others to contend with.

"Partner in the spa, eh?" Another man snorted. "Obviously, the bottom partner, *chivo!*" More bleating and snickering ensued, and they all looked at him sideways.

"*Vete a la mierda*, eh? I'm as straight as you are."

The guys gestured at him rudely and laughed. *Behhhh! Behhhh!* The animal noises got louder, the jeers more pronounced.

Alejo dished it right back. "What's the matter, guys? You having fond memories of the sheep you violated last night?"

"*Ooh*, Alejandro!" Luis ran up to him in a parody of a girlie skip. "I have a callous. Will you file it down for me, *por favor?*"

Alejo head-butted the ball right into his nose and grabbed himself in a very male, uncouth gesture. "*Jodete.* File down *this.*"

"Nothing there to file, since it melted in your boy-friend's mouth…" called another teammate.

"You want to say that again to me, within arm's length?" Alejandro asked him, menace in his voice. "Because I'll kick any ass on this field. What's more, you know I can do it. You're all free with the insults when there's fifteen against one. But will you meet me alone?"

"Asking for a date, Señor Manos?" A guy named Carlos mocked him.

"Date? Nah. Your mother begs me for it without me buying her dinner."

Carlos's face darkened and he clenched his fists. "What did you say?" He vaulted forward and threw a punch at Alejandro, who dodged it and knocked him right to the ground with a nice left hook.

Carlos was up again within seconds, raging for a good fight, but Franco pulled him back by the shirt collar. "*Detente!* You want to be infected with the *maricon's* blood?"

Alejandro gritted his teeth. This was going nowhere. They could trade insults—or punches—all night. He needed a different strategy.

Alejandro shouted, "How big is your mortgage? How much do you have to pay off in student loans? Business loans?"

"Eh?" Carlos stared at him, nonplussed by the change in subject. "A lot."

"Yes? Well, me, too. Except that I've paid my loans

down already fifty percent in one year—yes, by giving pedicures."

All the men snickered again. Then they stared at him, stone-faced.

He kept going. "And how do you, Jorge, hold yourself above me when you're working for The Man? Somebody orders you around all day while you kiss his ass. *I* have my own business."

Jorge's fleshy face suffused with red.

Alejandro took yet a different tack: "And you, Luis. Your family's in the restaurant business. Did you feel shame when you worked there as a waiter?"

Luis shook his head reluctantly.

"Well, my family was in the salon business. And I'm not ashamed of having worked there, either. So you can all shut the hell up, and you can come ask me for a job when my place is franchised all over the country. Maybe I'll hire you to mop floors or do shampoos."

Alejo skewered them all with his gaze. They still wore smirks, but at least the bleating and catcalling had stopped. "Now, do you want to practice, or not? Or are you still afraid—like a bunch of girls—that because of my *temporary* job, I'll take you from behind?"

Luis laughed outright at that, and Alejandro knew, though there was a long road ahead and still a lot of ribbing to come, that he'd won.

"Pass me the ball, *rosquete*." Luis said, finally. "Let's go!"

# 22

KATE LAY IN bed with T-bone and thought about the fact that she should be working. But she just couldn't force herself to pick her head up off the pillow. It was stuck there like a ten-pound filing to a magnet.

This probably had something to do with a very lowering realization: that she'd gone and fallen in love with Alejandro Torres, the lying sack of—

She rolled over and sighed. Why hadn't she fallen in love with Drexel, or Kippy or Stone? Someone who wasn't so impossibly good-looking and sexy. Someone who didn't wear a gold chain around his neck, insult her and make her buy girlie shoes. Someone whom she didn't want to punch and kiss at the same time.

She lifted her head with difficulty and smacked her pillow in the hopes of…something or other. She didn't know what. It just felt good to hit something.

It should have been Kippy, she decided. In spite of his somewhat bulbous eyes and his annoying habit of quoting statistics and reciting chemical compounds. Kippy had been nice and malleable, as long as she'd let him run his mouth.

She should have married Kippy when she had the

chance. Then she'd never have moved to Miami and met the smooth-talking Latin scourge of her existence.

But then she'd never have experienced really great sex. And she wouldn't have discovered how adorable and intelligent a pig could be. And she wouldn't have fallen in love.... Wait.

Falling in love belonged in the Con list, not the Pro list. It had knocked the breath out of her, as well as the sense. And even if it hadn't hurt at first, it sure as hell did now.

She made a conscious decision to fall *out* of love with him. Immediately. All it would take was a little willpower, damn it.

T-bone was obviously chasing something very exciting in her sleep, since her legs whirred like an egg-beater and she emitted snoozy little barks and whimpers as she almost caught it.

When the phone rang Kate ignored it, but after it stopped it just started ringing again. And again. Then her cell phone started, and wouldn't stop, either. It was a bloody cacophony of ring tones, and she finally fell out of bed with a curse and answered her main line. The phone with the caller ID was in the kitchen, so she couldn't tell who it was, and it might be some awful emergency.

It was someone awful, but not an emergency. "Katy! Damn you, I can't believe you did this to me!"

Huh? She pushed the hair out of her eyes and then said calmly, "Wendell, I have no idea what you're talking about."

"Don't play dumb, Katy. I will get you for this." His venom shot through the phone line.

Kate was mystified. "Wendell, again, I don't know what you're talking about. Will you at least tell me what I'm accused of? Because I'm honestly in the dark here."

"You have the nerve to tell me you had nothing to do with that *creature* bursting into my meeting and demanding that I live up to my promise to pay for her breast implants and buttock lift? Not to mention a sex-change operation?"

"What? Oh, Wendell! That sounds just awful. How embarrassing for you."

"And screeching that she'd serviced me enough times to pay off the national debt?" Wendell's voice shook with rage.

"Well, is it true?"

"No! You know it's not true! You set the whole thing up."

Someone had finally decided to repay Wendell's nastiness, but it wasn't her. She almost wished it had been. Kate bit her lip hard enough that she tasted the salty, metallic tang of blood. She couldn't laugh, not with him on the phone.

"Wendell, I assure you that I had nothing to do with the incident. I'm shocked and appalled."

He snarled.

"But you should always keep your promises," she added, unable to resist. "It's a point of honor with us Spinneys. You know that. So if you did promise to pay for her cosmetic surgery and sex change, you really should."

She could almost hear the flecks of foam spattering

his receiver as he struggled for words. "Bitch!" he finally screamed.

"There is no need for name-calling. I really didn't do this." *But I should have.*

"I've been fired from the Miami project because of this, you whore!"

"Wendell, we both know that with the trust, I don't need payment for sex. So I'm just a garden-variety slut. Now, honestly, this conversation is getting tiresome. I didn't have *anything* to do with this situation. I swear it. Why don't you pour yourself a nice double scotch and you'll feel better in the morning."

Kate hung up on the ear-splitting squeal of rage that followed her recommendation. In case he called back, she unplugged her house phone and turned off her cell. Then, unable to help herself, she laughed until tears rolled down her cheeks and her ribs hurt.

She pumped a fist into the air. "Somebody got that little rodent but good. I only wish I knew who it was."

T-bone opened one eye and wagged her tail.

"Maybe it will teach him a lesson."

T-bone looked dubious about that.

"Yeah, you're probably right." Kate went back to bed and relapsed into her state of depression.

She'd been an utter fool, and she was mortified, though still furious at Alejandro for lying to her. In fact, it was possible that she was even angrier, since his lie had led to her wrong conclusion in the first place, and therefore her foolishness and mortification was all his fault.

Kate told herself that the probabilities were the same:

so maybe he hadn't had a specific product in mind when he began to schmooze and romance her, but her name and financing couldn't hurt his business.

A small niggling voice told her that she wasn't being fair. But then a person who had consumed three pans of brownies in three days—plus one bowl of brownie batter—probably had sugar poisoning and couldn't be held to normal standards of fairness.

"Isn't that so, T-bone?"

The dog rolled over and placed her paw against Kate's cheek, very gently. She began to cry.

T-bone sat up, shook herself, and then began to lick the tears off Kate's face, which made her cry even harder. "I hate him, T."

She sat up in bed and wiped her face with her sleeve. "Yeah, if you want to know the God's honest truth, it would be a little embarrassing to introduce him to my family as my boyfriend, the macho male manicurist. But hell, why is it any *more* manly for my dad to be the CEO of a bloody shampoo company? I don't notice that he goes out of his way to talk about the tampon division at cocktail parties..." She sniffed. "So the whole thing is stupid!"

T-bone farted.

Kate nodded. "Yeah! It does stink. The whole situation stinks. But I'm not damn well apologizing to some jerk who lies to me and lets me believe he's an accountant!"

T-bone rolled over and licked at her stitches.

"Don't do that, sweetie. Picking at a wound only makes it worse."

The dog raised her head and looked at Kate for a long moment, her eyes warm and liquid and wise.

"You're right," Kate said finally, with a sigh. "We should get out of this dark bedroom and go for a walk."

"SHE'S GOT SOME nerve!" Alejandro shouted to Marly. "I will *not* apologize first. She thought I romanced her for her money! How insulting is that?"

Peggy, who stood in the corner of the kitchenette with them, sighed. "Well, you did lie to her, Alejo."

"I didn't lie, exactly. I omitted." He folded his arms across his chest and clamped his hands in his pits.

"You lied," Marly said matter-of-factly. "You said Señor Manos was a Peruvian product."

"He is," Alejandro insisted.

His two partners exchanged a long glance. He was getting really tired of that. They'd conspired against him from the beginning, these two.

"What?" he bellowed.

Peggy shoved a hand through her hair. "You're both idiots. And you're both wrong. So you're perfect for each other."

"I know that." Alejandro glared at her.

"But if neither one of you apologizes, then you're at an impasse." Marly stated the obvious. "By the way, she never wants to see you again, except to kill you."

"Great. Unfortunately, we have classes together. And we have the damned marketing project to pull together, too."

"E-mail," Peggy said, "is a wonderful thing."

He glowered at her. Then he stalked into the office and closed the door, glaring at the computer.

Ms. SPINNEY, KATE read later when she checked her e-mail, still in her pajamas.

As you are aware, the marketing project is due next Friday. Please find attached the spreadsheet and cost analysis you requested.
A.T.

Glaring at the screen, she typed back:

Mr. Torres,
I am fully aware of when the marketing project is due. I am in receipt of the spreadsheet and cost analysis. They look quite competent, considering they were executed by someone who is not, after all, an accountant.
However, I do not find attached an apology. It must have gotten lost in cyberspace.
K.S.

Ten minutes later she had his response:

Ms. Spinney,
You must be right. However, I have checked the stored documents on my computer, and cannot find the apology in question, so I'm unable to attach it. Many things do, of course, disappear in cyberspace: things such as trust and human emotion. Amazing, though, how *sheer gall* never seems to get lost.

If you should unearth an apology in your own files,
please, by all means send it.
A.T.

She lost no time in sending her reply:

Like hell.

Faster than electricity, he responded, too.

Stiff-necked little Yankee *bruja*.
Give me five minutes with you naked on a mattress,
and I'll have you begging me to let you apologize.

Kate spit her coffee onto the keyboard. *Bastard!*
While she wiped the N, M, space bar and alt keys with
a paper towel, she tried to think of a suitably withering
response, but her brain seemed to be malfunctioning.
Probably because the thought of being naked on a
mattress with Alejandro was rather distracting. Jerk!

For example, there were his broad shoulders to
consider, and the gorgeously sculpted muscles of his
biceps, triceps and forearms, lightly dusted with dark,
masculine hair.

*Yeah, the big, dumb primate.*

Not to mention the terrain of his chest, with those
flat, coppery nipples and defined six-pack, his flat
stomach and, lower down, his heavy, thick—

*Stop it!* She scolded herself. *Any horse is well-hung,
too. It doesn't mean the animal is fit to be ridden, much
less kept in your stable.*

And his legs. God, Alejandro's legs. Long, hard and packed with defined muscle. Legs that seemed oh, so talented at tangling with her own and prying her knees apart.

*Yeah, and probably all of his bosomy customers' knees, too.*

The way he spoke soft Spanish to her in bed, and caressed her jaw and the backs of her ears and her scalp. He could have her ready for him without even touching her below the neck—and that took serious talent.

*Gah! He is Satan. He lied to you about his job—so what else is he lying about?*

Kate stalked back to the computer with her answer for Alejandro. Stabbing each key, she wrote back.

I'd rather ride my broomstick and get splinters. Give me five minutes naked on a mattress with you, and you'll be a gelding!

# 23

ALEJANDRO DIDN'T HAVE any intention of giving Kate
warning. No, by God, he'd catch her completely unaware, and to do that he had to bypass the main entrance
where the kid named Kevin would force him to wait
while he called her unit.

Instead, Alejo remembered the freight elevator
they'd used to take Gracious down to the beach one
night. He walked around the building and found a back
entry which, conveniently, some maintenance worker
had wedged open with a brick. He slipped inside. Geld
him, she'd threatened? They'd just see about that.

He reached her floor and stalked to her door, rapping
on it with no hesitation.

"Who is it?" Kate's voice called warily.

"Pizza guy."

"You!" she said, furiously. She threw open the door and
stood resplendent in a scruffy white T-shirt and pajama
bottoms with mallards on them. "What do you want?"

"I'm here to be gelded, Kate."

"What?"

"Five minutes on a mattress, we agreed. And see, I
even brought you a Swiss Army knife. Your choice of

straight or serrated blades. There's even a small scissors in it." He grinned and pressed it into her hand.

"You're *insane*."

He nodded. "Definitely, most men would consider me insane. Now come along, Kate." He poked her in the stomach with an index finger and when she didn't move, he shrugged and pushed past her, whipping off his shirt and kicking off his shoes.

T-bone growled at him and bristled.

"Yeah, well, I brought you something, too." Alejo reached into his pocket and took out a dog treat.

"Don't you dare take that, T-bone!" Kate snapped. To him, she said, "Get out."

T-bone eagerly gobbled the treat and wagged her tail, sniffing around for more.

Alejandro unbuckled his belt with one hand and scratched the dog behind the ears with the other one.

"What in the hell do you think you're doing?"

"Five minutes naked on a mattress," he said again, patiently. "We agreed. It's even in writing."

"I agreed to nothing," she declared, as he dropped his pants. "Put those back on, damn it!"

He smirked at her and dropped his drawers, standing completely nude in front of her, and with a healthy erection, too. He swiveled his hips so it waggled at her.

She turned her back on him, shaking with emotion.

"So which will it be, *mi corazon?* I'd very much prefer that you not use the scissors. That would take a long time, and they'd probably be irreparably blunt afterwards."

She hunched forward, shaking even harder and let out something that sounded like a sob. He frowned and was at her side in an instant, all seriousness. "What is it, *mi amor?* I'm sorry—I did not mean to make you cry!"

Her body wracked with new spasms and he started to get alarmed. Then she finally raised her head and he saw her face, contorted with mirth. She could hardly breathe, she was laughing so hard. Finally she made a sound somewhat like a donkey in labor and went into more convulsions of giggles while he grinned back at her. He *was* a pretty funny guy, if he did say so himself.

When she caught her breath, leaning over with her hands braced on her knees, she said, "Hah."

"Hah?"

"You *apologized!*" she declared in triumphant tones.

"I did no such thing."

"You did! You just did! You said, '*I'm sorry, mi amor.*'"

He scoffed. "That's when I thought you were crying. It doesn't count."

"It most certainly does."

"No, it does not."

"Look, do you want to be friends again or not?"

"What I want is my five minutes on the mattress."

"That is *so* not going to happen, sport."

"You are obviously afraid of succumbing to my masculine charms, *mi amor.*" He smirked at her.

"Oh, please." She turned her back on him again, which was a mistake. He de-pantsed her in a single fluid motion and saw with great satisfaction that she wore no panties under her pajama bottoms.

"Hey!"

Then he picked her up, the jammies still twined

around one of her ankles, and rubbed the length of himself between her legs. She was slick for him already and he made the mistake of permitting himself a smug smile as he slowly slid inside her to the hilt.

Though he knew very well that she'd enjoyed the sensation as much as he had, she pulled off of him in a single fluid motion. "I sure hope that felt good to you, sport, because that's the only taste of it you're going to get. Now put me down."

*Bruja.* Little *flauta.* "Oh, yes?" he asked softly. He made a single motion of his own, transferring all of her weight to his left arm, leaving his right hand free to play. He reached beneath her, awkward as it was, and maneuvered his fingers along the slippery cleft between her legs. He slipped them back and forth rapidly and then found the small nub at her very center, circling it gently and then stroking it.

"Stop that," she said, but her voice began to lack conviction.

"A gentleman always obliges," he said. He shoved her shirt up and bent his head to her breasts instead.

"Put me down," she told him, faintly.

Alejo walked into the bedroom with her and set her at the edge of the mattress, but remained between her legs. He stripped off her mangy T-shirt so that he could have better access to her breasts, which were now jutting forward and pebbled at the tips. He took one in his mouth and sucked, hard.

"I really don't like you very much," Kate said, on the crest of a moan.

"I don't like you much, either," Alejo told her, taking

the other breast into his mouth. "But we've got to get through five minutes naked on this mattress. Now, are you still inclined to geld me?"

She reached down and grabbed his rascal, wrapping her hands around it snugly. She shook her head.

"What are you planning to do with that?"

She guided it to where she wanted it to go.

Though it just about killed him, he removed her hands and shook his head. "No, no. I've had my one stroke, remember? I'm trying not to be greedy, *mi amor.*"

She cussed weakly at him and he gave her an insolent smile. "I've got something we could clean out your dirty mouth with, though."

Kate bared her teeth at him.

"On second thought," he mused, "we could just get mine dirty instead." He pushed her thighs apart so that they were almost parallel to the side of the mattress, and took his time for a moment, enjoying the view.

Then he swooped down and took her with his mouth in a single motion. She gave a small scream of pleasure, writhing under his tongue.

"Like that, *mi corazon?*" he laughed softly, scraping his five o'clock shadow along her inner thigh.

She moaned. "Yes."

"But you want my cock in you even more."

"Yes," she admitted, flushing with embarrassment.

He bent his head and teased her some more. "You want it fast and hard? Or slow and sweet?" He maneuvered his hands under her bottom, squeezing a warm cheek in each.

She raised her hips. "H-hard."

"Yes?" He stabbed his tongue inside her and then raised his head again. "Well, you give me a fast, hard apology, and then I'll give it to you that way."

She froze and he watched with amusement as she gritted her teeth. Pride fought a duel with lust all over her face.

"Screw you," she said.

He chuckled as she made an attempt to wriggle back and away from him, and held her still while he slid his tongue over her, back and forth, until she was panting and gripping his skull.

"Are you sorry, Kate? That you doubted my motives and accused me of being a scumbag?" He went in for the kill, a figure-eight maneuver with a flutter at the center.

"*Haaaaaaaaah*," she gasped, shaking all over, but this time not with mirth.

"Want me inside, baby? One little word. That's all it takes."

"S-sorry!"

"*Thank you*," he said, standing and driving into her tight heat. She convulsed around him at once, thrashing under him helplessly.

Then she added, "You lying rat bastard."

SOME TIME LATER, Kate opened her eyes and looked at Alejandro. "If your apology doesn't count, then neither does mine."

"Yours definitely counts," he said, rolling over. "You yelled it. There was a lot of remorse behind that *sorry*, judging by volume alone."

She squinted at him. "There was *not*. It was given under circumstances of coercion."

"Mmm," he said, his expression happily reminiscent. "I could always make you apologize to me again...."

She figured she'd better not argue with him. "Look," she told him severely. "Let's just call this a draw. You don't apologize to me for being a lying creep, and I won't apologize to you for thinking you were pond scum. We'll forget that I'm mostly right because you really were lying to me...."

His face had darkened and she hastily moved out of his grasp. "And I'll tell you about my absolutely brilliant marketing solution for After Hours."

"First, Ms. Spinney, let's clear the air between us, apologies or not. I couldn't give a crap about your money, and you can invest it in flamingo racing for all I care. Second, there are so many damned things that Spinneys won't or don't do that I wouldn't want to be connected to them in any way. And third, the only reason I lied to you is that I didn't want to be less of a man in your eyes. Got it?"

She finally nodded. "I think it's ridiculous, but I guess I understand, you being such a big, macho lunkhead. Now, will you let me tell you my marketing idea? It's truly ingenious."

"No false modesty about you, Kate, is there?" he teased. "At least when it comes to ideas."

"I don't understand," she complained. "In Boston, we're supposed to hide our breasts and display our intellect. In Miami, it's the reverse!"

He laughed. "Go on. Tell me all about your genius."

When she was finished, he simply stared at her. Then he fell on the floor laughing. And finally, he seized her and kissed her until she could barely breathe.

"Kate, *mi corazon,* this is why I romanced you—not only for your beauty but for your mind. Though how anyone can be so knot-headed and brilliant at the same time, I'll never understand."

"It takes real talent," she told him.

"Yes, I know." Alejandro rubbed his knuckles gently over her cheekbones, and the realization he'd been avoiding rushed him and knocked him down.

He was one hundred percent in love with this maddening woman. He sat there reeling with the sudden discovery, and finally cleared his throat. "That's why I want you forever—for your many talents."

Kate actually blushed. "You want me forever?"

He looked deep into her eyes and nodded, then tucked her hair behind her ears. "I love you."

She absorbed that, knitting her eyebrows. "You do? Are you sure?"

"Yes, I'm sure. You bring out the moron and the caveman in me. That's how I know. With other women, I'm suave. With you, I just want to toss you over my shoulder and drag you back to my lair and keep you naked."

"Are you *proposing* to me, Alejandro?"

That caught him off guard, but he thought about it. He cocked his head to one side. "Would you hit me if I did?"

"Probably." Kate grinned at him. "I'm a feminist, remember? We don't get into all that mushy stuff."

"Then how am I ever going to achieve my fantasy of being a kept man?"

She laughed and kissed him before saying the words he most wanted to hear. "Alejandro, I love you, too."

*Yes!*

"But…I don't know if I'm ready to get married. Can I keep you without papers?"

To tell the truth, he didn't know if he was ready to get married, either. This was all a little sudden. "For a while. But only if you wear my gold chain. It will mark you as mine, all mine."

Kate looked repelled for a moment, before her face split into a dazzling smile. "Deal! It's a deal. Oh, cool. And I thought I'd *never* get that tacky necklace off you…."

# *Epilogue*

*One Year Later*

AFTER HOURS OVERFLOWED with people of every age, sex and lifestyle, and most of them were dancing. If they refrained from toe-tapping, then they laughed long and loudly. And if they didn't dissolve into mirth, they flirted wildly and spent buckets of money.

Alejandro still couldn't quite believe it. They'd been popular before, with a good crowd most nights, but this went beyond all expectations. He caught Kate's eye across the room, and she grinned, her hair as messy as it had ever been in spite of Marly's best efforts to tame it.

He loved her crazy hair. As much as he loved her.

He wanted to marry her. He really did. The realization hit him in the face, along with Heather Carlton's pink lizard handbag.

"Hey, Romeo. I was *talking* to you," she said.

"Uh. Sorry, *mi amorcito.* I was trying to see if they needed anything behind the bar." Not that anyone could see the bar at the moment....

"Well, I was asking you a question. I know you, um, have certain feelings for me, and I wanted to let you down easy, but—" She heaved a deep and dramatic sigh which jiggled her considerable pink cleavage.

Could it be? Was he about to be paroled from Heather Carlton without offending her? He'd dreaded announcing his retirement to her for fear she'd take it personally.

She glanced quickly behind her to the long row of pedicure stations, each manned by a big, strapping young man in a muscle shirt. "But I'm switching to Raoul."

Praise God and all His angels! Alejandro clapped a hand to his heart. "I don't know what to say." He swallowed, bent his head and then raised his chin again, taking a deep, stoic gulp of air. "I am devastated."

"I feel really bad," said Heather.

Alejandro put out a hand, palm forward. "I know." He took another deep breath. "I will recover. I will…get over it. Go to him. Be happy."

As Heather minced away, Alejandro blessed Kate over and over, for recommending to him that After Hours hire only gorgeous hunks to do their pedicures from now on, and pay them double as incentive to get over the macho issue.

The clientele—ninety percent female anyway—had tripled since then, and they were already opening two new locations to accommodate all the desperate housewives—and tired female executives—out there.

The music behind him reached a crescendo and the feet thundering on the bar stopped as the Brazilian pop song ended. His guys weren't stupid, and they knew they got better tips as their shirts got tighter and the bulges in their pants got more pronounced.

Alejo hid a smile as he spied both Shirlie and Nicky with huge wads of dollar bills, evaluating the gyrating bulges. Did they have no shame?

He happened to know that a couple of the guys employed rolled tube socks, but if it excited the customers and his gullible staff, then why should he care? He laughed when he saw a couple of the Fab Four hoisting themselves up onto the bar. He made his way over there with some difficulty. "Don't let either of them fall," he admonished one of the bartenders. "And if someone has to drive them home later, make it Esteban."

He picked his way through the crowd, searching for Kate, and marveled again at the crowd. This was far better than the A they'd gotten from Professor Kurtz. This was pure gold—and it hadn't only been Kate's doing. He smiled with pride. No, it had been his idea to turn After Hours into a real bar—with the added benefits of salon and spa facilities.

Peggy's fiancé, Troy, owned the whole strip mall, and had made it possible for them to take over the business next door and knock down the wall between the two spaces. After Hours stayed open now until 2:00 a.m. and served hard alcohol, another reason the money continued to pour in.

Marly, engaged to Governor Jack Hammersmith, was boogying down with him in a corner while a photographer stalked them without subtlety.

Peggy and Troy were MIA, but Alejo had noticed a flickering light under the back treatment room door, and nobody was scheduled for a massage with her tonight. He grinned. Now he *really* wanted to find Kate.

His grin disappeared as he saw Tia Carlotta dressed in something low-cut and red, dancing much too close to that damned tree man. He pushed his way through the crowd until he got to her. "Tia, may I speak to you for a moment?"

She rolled her eyes and told *Stan* that she'd be right back.

"Tia, what are you doing here?"

"Checking on my investment," she said, hands on her hips. Her bright red lipstick was a bit smeared, and Alejo shuddered as he thought about how it might have gotten that way. The possibility that his aunt might have a sex life revolted him.

"Why is Stan the tree man here with you?"

She dimpled and fanned herself with one hand. "Eh? Stan—he come to make sure he got all the, how you say, roots out of ground."

*I'll just bet he did.*

"He grind the stump," she said, patting her hair. Was that henna in it?

*And what else is he grinding?* Alejandro cast a suspicious glance toward Stan.

"He *loooove*," Tia purred, "my *cau-cau*."

"You're feeding some tree guy now, instead of me?"

"Why not, eh? You eat with that *gringa* now." She wrinkled her nose. Tia was not partial to Kate, as he'd feared, and the feeling was mutual.

"But she feeds the steak to the dog, not me!" He still hadn't gotten over that.

"Alejo, this is no my *problema*. Manuela, God rest her soul, would want me to find happiness. Now, I get back to dancing, yes?"

"Tia, I thought you hated the idea of me turning the salon into a bar. You said it would never work. You said you wanted to pull your money out, and predicted degenerate behavior here!"

"I never say such thing. Manuela, God rest her soul, would not want you making up stories. Now, Alejandro, you get me a mojito, eh? Your Tia is dying with thirst." And she pinched his cheek and gyrated away to Stan the tree man, who eyed his Tia's backside in a way that made Alejo want to take him down and grind *his* stump.

However, she probably wouldn't thank him for that, so he shook off his disgust and made his way toward the bar again.

A high-pitched shriek rent his eardrums and he looked toward the source of it. To his amusement Kate was being pulled up forcibly onto the bar by two big male dancers.

"No!" she said. "No, no, no!" They laughed and hauled her up anyway. They sandwiched her between them, doing a little shimmy.

"No, really!" she shouted, crossly, her wiry hair standing on end. "Spinneys do *not* dance on bars…" Then she stopped, an arrested expression on her face. "Alejandro, I need a table," she yelled. "A small round one."

"Why? Are you going to serve tea in my bar?"

"Not exactly," said his love, a smile playing under those killer cheekbones of hers. "There's something I swore I'd do before my thirtieth birthday, but I didn't quite make it."

Puzzled, Alejandro went to the back of the bar, where he saw Luis, Carlos and Franco sitting around a small table and testing their ability to hold tequila. Luis winked and hoisted a shot glass to him. "Eh, Chivo!"

"That's Señor Chivo to you, my friend." And so saying, he plucked their table right out from under them, dropping the tequila bottle into Franco's lap.

He strode back to the front of the bar with his prize, placing it in front of Kate. "Your table awaits, *señorita*."

She gulped and then hesitated. "Will you put me on it, please?"

Highly entertained, he caught her around the waist, lifted her and set her on the tabletop. Around them people started whistling and clapping.

Kate stood stock-still for a long moment, twin spots of color riding high on her cheekbones. Then she tucked her crazy hair behind her ears and began to dance. She moved her hips and her shoulders, her knees and her feet. She tossed her head and raised her hands into the air, finally whooping in exultation.

"I thought Spinneys didn't make public spectacles of themselves!" Alejandro shouted up at her.

"They don't," she answered, grinning. "But sometimes Just Kate does."

"Brava!"

"Of course, my family would consider this highly indecent," she told him as he swung her down.

"It was your brilliant marketing idea to have the guys dancing on the bar for clients. You're just encouraging them, that's all. It's part of your job."

She made a face at him.

"Speaking of indecency," he continued with a wicked

grin, "I really think we should check on the inventory in the supply closet. Don't you?"

"I don't think that's necessary, Alejandro."

He pulled her close so that she could see just how necessary it was. "Really, I think we're low on, uh, shampoo."

"You are *so* transparent."

"Yes, but I am cute, no?" Alejandro took her hand and tugged her behind him to the supply closet, but curiously it was locked. "Damn. I'll have to go and find the key."

Muffled laughter came from inside the closet. Then a familiar female voice said, "Alejo, you open this door and I will bleach your hair while you sleep."

"Yeah," came another voice, this one deep and masculine. "And I'll pass a bill making it illegal for you to get a hard-on anywhere in the state of Florida."

Marly and Jack had pre-empted them!

They tried the office next, but soft moans and rustling came from behind that door, too. What the hell? Tia Carlotta's prediction had come true. After Hours was hosting some serious hanky-panky.

"Fine." Alejandro gritted his teeth. "Then it will have to be the bathroom."

"Spinneys," declared Kate, "do *not* do it in bathrooms."

"Spinneys," said Alejandro, "will do it anywhere we can, and if the bathroom is occupied, I think we are down to the Dumpster."

"What is the matter with you? You're crazy. I'm not having sex with you in the garbage."

"Did I ask you to have sex with me in the garbage?"

He threw up his hands. "No, I did not. All I wanted to do was find a somewhat private place to tell you that I have to insist on marrying your bony, snooty, uptight little ass!"

Kate blinked at him. "Oh. Really?"

"Yes, really. Though that is not the way I meant to phrase it…."

She reached up to touch the muscle jumping in his jaw. "That's okay. Spinneys don't do sappy public proposals, either." She looked around, but nobody was paying any attention to them. "So, keep it quiet. I might even say yes, since I've gotten kind of attached to you. Only for the free pedicures, of course."

He bent to kiss her. "Kate Spinney, will you marry a former male manicurist? With a prenuptial agreement, of course."

The very unsentimental apple of his eye actually got tears in hers, to his surprise. "Yeah, I would. If you'd consider marrying a vice president of either tampons or wart cream."

He burst out laughing. "Excuse me?"

"Really," she said seriously. "Wendell's just been put in charge of the hemorrhoid and suppository products up in Boston, which leaves me the choice of the other two. Spinney Industries is moving them to the Miami division."

He looked down into her green eyes and frowned. "I thought you said you were a *shampoo* heiress, Kate."

She squirmed. "Well…the company really did start with shampoo, back in 1914. But let's just say it's diversified a lot, and our branch of the family is in charge of the more embarrassing stuff. I kind of omitted to tell you that."

He grasped her by the arms, wanting very badly to shake her until her teeth rattled. *This* was the woman who'd given him hell for not being straight with her? The woman who'd demanded an abject apology from him for lying—and taken it, too, when it had only been accidental?

He was going to wring her snotty, East Coast little neck. "Let me get this straight. Are you saying that—" Words failed him.

Her green gaze slid away from his, and then she squinted up at him hopefully, lip caught between her teeth. "Oh, come on, sport. It was just a *little* white lie. An omission, that's all. Now, what kind of engagement party do you want to have?"